I0747285

POUR decisions

Katrina Marie

This one is for the Hubs. You bugged me for a rose when we were fourteen on the bus ride home. Who knew less than ten years later we'd finally get our chance.

prologue

. . .

THIS IS SO EMBARRASSING. I thought for sure my parents would stop this tradition after elementary school. Everybody on the bus will give me crap because of the ginormous vase of flowers I'm carrying with me.

I sling my backpack over my shoulder and grab the flowers off my desk. Days like today, I wish my parents picked me up for school. Maybe I'll ask if we can do that. Besides, we'd get home faster, which means I could do my chores and help with the winery sooner than later. Not that I do much, mostly help move the bottles before they are filled, but still…

My bus pulls in front of the school, and I rush outside from the small corner I'm hiding in. A single file line is in front of the doors. Maybe I should have been waiting outside. At this rate, I'll have to share a seat with someone.

"Good afternoon, Piper." The driver nods her head toward me as I step onto the bus. "Those are some beautiful flowers you've got there. Any special occasion?"

I can feel my cheeks heat, but I smile. At least our bus

driver loves us and knows who we are. "It's my birthday. My parents give me flowers every year."

"Well, happy birthday."

"Thank you."

I glance down the aisle to see if there are any open seats. Just my luck, all the seats at the front are full. I move toward the back, searching. There's a seat that looks empty. I hurry my steps, only to find it occupied. There's a boy slumped down in the seat, holding a book.

There are groans coming from behind me, and I know I need to find a place to sit soon. There are a few more seats at the very back, but the kids who sit there don't like when others take them. I'd rather not have a confrontation on my birthday.

"Can I sit with you?"

The boy doesn't make a move. Maybe he didn't hear me. It is kind of loud in here.

"Excuse me," I tap him on the shoulder. "Can I sit with you?"

He glances up and at the vase in my hands. "Sure, but you sit by the window."

Fine by me. I prefer that to getting bumped every time a kid gets off the bus. "Thank you."

I wait for him to move out of the seat so I can scoot in. My parents didn't think this delivery through very well. How am I supposed to hold my backpack and these flowers in my lap?"

"Here." The boy holds out his hand once he's seated next to me. "Let me hold those so you can put your bag down."

"Thanks." I slide my bag to the floor between my feet. The last thing I want is for it to go sliding every time we go around a curve. It's bound to happen since we live on country roads.

He hands me the flowers and I place them on my lap. I study the boy around my flowers. Thank goodness I have them to hide behind.

He's reading his book again. It looks like a mystery book, but I can't tell because his hand is covering the title.

I don't recognize him. He looks like he's in my grade, but we live in a small town. There are maybe a hundred people in my class. I would have seen him at some point.

He must feel my eyes on him because he turns toward me. "Is there something you need?"

"Oh, no." I smile. "Are you new here? I haven't seen you before."

He folds the corner of the page down and closes his book. A tiny part of me winces at the action. Does he not own a bookmark?

"We just moved here last week. Today's my first day riding the bus." He points to the flowers I'm holding. "Are you celebrating something?"

"It's my birthday." This time the words come out easier. He may have sounded rude when I first sat down, but he did close his book to engage in conversation with me. "I'm Piper, by the way."

"My name is Beau." He gives me a little wave.

I'm glad he didn't try to shake my hand. It's something I see my dad do all the time, and it feels like something only adults do. Besides, it's not like I can really let go of this vase without dropping it. The roads on the way home aren't horrible, but they aren't great, either.

"Where do you live? It's probably near me since we're on the same bus route."

"I live on Starlit Road."

"Me, too." I grin at him. "My family owns the winery at the end of the road."

"Oh cool." He nods and thinks for a second. "I guess that means we're neighbors. We moved into the house next door."

"Awesome, we'll have to hang out sometime."

He doesn't say anything for a few moments, and I fear I may have scared him off already. It's not that I don't have friends, but their parents don't want to have to drive more than ten minutes to bring them over unless I'm having a sleepover. It would be nice to have someone to hang out with who won't have that problem.

"I'd like that." He smiles. "So, do I get to have one of those roses?"

"Absolutely not." I hug them tighter to me as I laugh. "I happen to like my roses."

Yes, I was complaining about having to carry them on the bus, but I do love them. There's just something about fresh flowers in my room that makes the days brighter.

"That's cool."

The bus turns onto our road and I'm shocked I haven't realized the other stops. Talking to Beau has made the ride more bearable than usual. The bus gets down to the end of the road and opens the doors.

"This is us." I glance at my flower and my bag, trying to figure out how I'm going to do this without spilling water everywhere.

Beau stands and slings his backpack over his shoulder before grabbing my flowers. That was thoughtful. I bend down to get my bag and follow him off the bus.

Once we're both off, he points to my house. "I'll walk you home and carry these for you."

"Thank you."

We spend the next few minutes talking about the music we listen to and what we like to do in our free time. He's really easy to talk to, and nothing like my brothers and sister.

"I think I have it from here."

We're at the end of my driveway. I'm not sure how my dad will take a boy walking me home. Especially one he's never met.

"I'll see you at school tomorrow." He gives an awkward wave before turning in the direction of his house.

I pull a rose out of my vase. "Wait!"

He stops and faces me. "What are you doing?"

"Giving you a rose. Think of it as a symbol of our brand new friendship."

I place it in his hands, careful to make sure he still has a hold on it, and isn't getting pricked by a thorn.

"Thank you." He lifts it up in goodbye before walking to his house. I can already tell we're going to be best friends.

one

. . .

piper

ONE LAST CHECK. The notecards are in a stack by my laptop. I grab the cord connected to my laptop and follow it to the projection screen. One of these days I'm going to talk Mom and Dad into getting something that can connect with bluetooth. If not, one of us will trip…and it'll likely be me.

I take a deep breath and let it out. I've got this. As soon as I'm done with this presentation, everyone will see the direction we need to go with our marketing. If we want to stay ahead of the other wine brands out there, we need to up our game. Would it be nice to not have to do all this work? Yes. It's just not going to take us where I know my brother wants the company to go, even if he won't admit it.

We've always been a small winery. The local bar and some stores carry our wines, but we need to get outside of

Texas and scale up to a national level. I'm hoping my ideas will pique their interest.

"You're here early." Pierce, my oldest brother, comes into the room and takes a seat at the table. "We usually have to call you a million times to get you here thirty minutes late."

I hold my hand out to him. "I'm not letting you ruin my good mood. I needed to make sure my presentation is ready to go for the weekly meeting."

"I didn't know this was on the agenda today." He looks at his phone and scrolls down the screen. "There's nothing there."

"Because you've deleted it every time I've added it to the document." Even though he's doing some things differently than Dad and Grandpa, he refuses to move in a direction that could lead to great returns. "Today, I'm not giving you that chance. And I want to go first. I don't want everyone to get bogged down from other things on your list and not listen to what I have to say."

He lifts his hand to his chin and taps it. The look is giving villain vibes and I'm not sure he realizes it. "Fine. You can do your presentation when everyone else gets here."

It's a minor victory, but I'll take it for what it is. I only hope they'll actually listen to what I have to say. Beau gave me a pep talk last night when I ran it by him. At least I have one person in my corner. It's too bad he doesn't work at the winery. I wonder if Paula would have my back. I'm almost certain she would. She's all about bucking the expectations our family had.

All I'm asking for is to be heard. That small act in itself would show me they value my opinion. Nobody ever takes me seriously since I'm the baby of the family. They know what's best because they have more experience. Or, that's what they think, anyway.

The rest of my siblings file into the meeting room and take their seats. Well, except Paula. She works at the local flower shop and only steps in with special events. I wish she were here right now. I could actually use her input for some of what I want to do.

Finally, Mom and Dad enter the room. Nerves zing through my entire body. They have to give me a chance, right? I guess there's only one way to find out.

"Piper has something she'd like to show us before we get started." Pierce announces to the room and leans on the table.

Did he have to make it sound like I'm a school kid giving a presentation? I swear he can be such an ass sometimes. He expects all of us to give him respect as the eldest brother, but doesn't return the sentiment unless he has to. Now, I really wish Paula was here. She's the only person who ever stands up to him. The rest of my siblings roll over whenever he says something.

I won't let his choice of words get to me, though. All that matters is showing my family my ideas. He's not the only one who gets to make decisions.

"There are a few things I think we could improve on when it comes to marketing Starlit Fields and our brand." I open my laptop and start the presentation.

"We're a small, family-owned winery and I think it's something we need to lean into. We also need to up our social media presence."

My dad opens his mouth, and Pierce is already shaking

his head. I don't know why because neither of them have to do a thing.

"That is something I'll handle. But we need to let possible customers know we exist outside of Texas. Running ads on billboards and word of mouth are great. But we'll never be a household name the way Pierce wants us to be unless we meet customers where they are, and that is in online spaces."

I flip through the next few slides showing them all the statistics of various sites and how many people scroll through them on a daily basis.

"We can always run ads on these sites, but I think if we take it a step further and show them what it's like to own a small business, we'll appeal to more people. They want to know the behind the scenes, and the people who are behind the product they love to consume. And, I'm the perfect person to lead this up."

It's not a lie. The amount of hours I spend on socials every day probably isn't good. But I've seen the way other small companies are showing up for their customer base, and if we don't step it up…our wines will never be the ones people grab first when there are a ton of different choices.

The room is silent. I glance around the table at each of my siblings, but they quickly look down. Suddenly their phones are more important. Except for Pierce. His attention hasn't left me once. The scrutiny is overwhelming, and I shift my attention to Dad.

His focus in on the last slide of the presentation I gave moments ago. I worry he isn't going to say anything, but finally, he does.

"I don't know, Piper." Dad sets his elbows on the table.

"All of this seems like a lot of work. Most of us don't want to have a presence online."

When he says that, I know he means him and Mom. They like to scroll to find animal memes, but they rarely post anything. Not that I blame them. They prefer the simpler life.

"Not everyone has to be the face of Starlit Fields. I can do most of it without even showing people what we look like, but I think it's best if we have at least one person the viewers get to know. I'm okay with that being me."

It's probably best that it's me anyway. I'm the bubbliest person in the family, aside from Parker. Actually, he would be a good fit as well. Maybe I can talk him into it if the rest of the family agrees to my plans.

There's no reason to say no. They won't have any extra work. It all falls on me. That has to account for something, right?

Pierce glances around the room, and I hold my breath. Dad has put most of the decision making on him since he'll be the boss soon. He has to see that this is a good direction to take the winery. Especially since he's all about growth. Though, I think he's hoping for it on a smaller scale. I'm thinking big picture.

"I appreciate the effort, Piper. I really do." He pauses and meets my eyes before continuing. "But I don't think right now is the time for it. We have to gear up for the busy season in Asheville."

"Seriously." I can't help the outburst. I make eye contact with each of my siblings before turning my focus on my big brother. "You were just talking about growing and trying new things on the family vacation. That's what I'm trying to do. We're never going to be a household name if we don't take some risks. It's not like I'm asking for money to do it. The only thing I need is time, and I have plenty of that."

"You already manage the social media page, and it does fine."

"But it could be so much better than still images of our wines against a backdrop with information that can be found on the bottle. Please, just give this a chance."

"I'm sorry, Piper. Now isn't the time."

Nor will it ever be if it's up to him. I close my laptop and turn off the screen before taking my seat at the table. What I really want to do is storm out. But I'm an adult. If I did that, they'd still see me as the baby of the family making a scene to get my way. I refuse to give Pierce the satisfaction.

I pull out my phone and open up the document he sends us every week for this meeting. One of these days he's going to realize I'm right.

All he's doing is rehashing things we talk about every week. I tune him out and brainstorm ways I can convince him to let me do what I need to. Finally, he stands and concludes the meeting.

Parker comes up to me after everyone else has left the room. "For what it's worth, I think your ideas are amazing. Pierce is letting his ego make his decisions."

"Yeah, he is." I shove my laptop into my bag. "But you could have had my back. Nobody ever listens to me, but with a little support from a couple of you, he probably would have said yes."

Parker laughs and leans against the wall. "You know damn well he wouldn't have budged. He's a lot like dad and stuck in his ways."

"You talk about him like he's an old man."

"Compared to the rest of us, he is. Maybe we should set him up on a date. That might mellow him out some."

"Oh my God, I wouldn't wish a night of boring torture on anyone. I think that might fall under cruel and unusual punishment." I sling my bag over my shoulder and head toward the door. "I'm going to lunch."

"Want company?"

Do I? Not really. If he had spoken up for me after my presentation, maybe. Right now, I need to be alone.

"No. I'll bring something back for you, though."

"Cool." He must have noticed my mood. He wraps me in a hug. "Next time I'll say something."

"Thanks."

Little does he know it's probably too little too late. Pierce won't give me another chance to ambush them. It's probably best if I let things settle for a bit anyway. I'll get another chance…eventually.

As soon as I open the door, heat blasts me. As much as I love summer, it'd be great if it wasn't a million degrees at any given point in the day. I get in my car and roll the windows down before turning it on and blasting the air conditioner.

It'll take a few minutes to cool down, but it gives me time to get my shit together. If I walk into Out of the Ashes in my current mood, there's no doubt the bartender, Eric, will try to pry information out of me. He's like an emotion detector and is determined to get to the bottom of whatever is ailing someone at the moment.

Too bad the only person who can cheer me up works an hour away. He needs a job in town so we can do lunch dates together. It would give me some reprieve when my family is doing everything in their power to squash my dreams.

But, no. Beau has to work for some fancy marketing firm. Doesn't he know best friends are supposed to be available whenever there's a problem. I can't do that with him so far away.

I pick up my phone to send him a text and put it down immediately. He doesn't need to worry about me while he's at work. He'll get all my frustrations soon enough.

two

. . .

beau

MY FINGERS SHAKE as I move the mouse on the computer screen. Why is it always so cold in this freaking office? The whole team looks at me weird because I come in wearing a hoodie despite it being a hundred degrees outside. Still, there's no reason to have it freezing in here. I think it might be time to invest in some hand warmers. Though, I'm sure I'll get shit for that, too.

"What are you working on?" Cole, one of the guys in the small business department, leans over my shoulder.

"You should probably get glasses if you have to get this close to see my screen." I push him away. "It's a proposal for my friend's winery. Well, it belongs to the family, but she's in charge of marketing."

"Why are there two of them? Unless my vision is really that bad and I'm seeing double."

This isn't something I want to get into. But, if I don't tell him, he won't leave. I swear, if I had the capital, I would have my own firm and I wouldn't have to deal with nosy coworkers.

"Because everything hinges on a presentation she's giving this morning. One is if they agree with her, the other is if they don't. It's complicated."

It's not. It's actually quite simple. She has an idea and the rest of her family shoots it down. Or, more precisely, her big brother does. Cole doesn't need to know all that. Besides, it's not my story to tell, even if I've basically been part of the family since I was thirteen.

"Well." He claps me on the back. "I'm glad I'm not you. Double the work for the same pay."

"We do what we have to in order to make the client happy."

Little does he know that if the rest of the Summers family is on board, Starlit Fields has the possibility of being a major client.

"I guess it helps when it's someone you know on a personal level."

"Yep."

Cole takes the hint and turns away from my desk. "I'll catch you later."

I wave dismissively behind me. He's not a bad guy, just driven. It doesn't help that he's the boss's nephew. I've even gotten drinks with him after work, but he doesn't know when it's time to drop a conversation. Or personal boundaries, for that matter. I haven't even introduced him to Piper. Outside of her, I don't have a ton of friends I go out with on the regular. She's been my rock for as long as I can remember, and I've never really needed anyone else.

I glance at the time on my phone. She should be done with

her presentation by now. The fact she hasn't sent me a text is worrisome. I don't want to assume things didn't go well, but I have a gut feeling. There's only one way to find out.

I keep my phone in my hand expecting a quick response, but it doesn't come, and I set it down. I guess I was wrong. Maybe they loved it, and Piper is going over all the details.

My focus shifts to the marketing plan on the right side of my screen. It has bullet points of everything she's mentioned in passing. Piper has some great ideas. Some of them I've seen social media influencers do, and I think they'd translate well to the winery. As long as she can make most of the content personal, she'll be golden.

I continue listing out a few other things we can do regarding social media, but also some ads I'd love to propose we run. I know they don't have a big budget, so I have to keep it at a small scale in the beginning. The social media campaign would help increase the amount of play money we have exponentially.

Excitement flows through me. Her family is finally listening to her. After all these years they see her as more than the baby sister. She's always been more than that. They've never really given her a chance to make a difference in the business side of the winery, but it's about time they are.

The screen on my phone lights up, and I finish adding another bullet point before I glance down at it.

PIPER

Can you come over tonight?

BEAU

Sure. Is everything okay?

PIPER

Ugh

That one word is all the answer I need. They didn't like her presentation. Hell, Pierce may not have given her time to show anything. I don't want to hash all that out over text messages. Mostly because I'm at work. While they don't have a strict policy on cell phones; they aren't fans of long personal calls. I have a feeling if I called her right now, we would be on the phone for an hour, minimum.

BEAU

I'll head straight to your house when I get off work.

I don't expect her to respond, and I set the phone back down. After saving all the work I just did for the Piper plan, I switch over to the Summers' plan. While there are some advertising costs involved, it's pretty bare bones, and I hope they like the idea.

Maybe I'll talk to them, since they won't take Piper seriously. Not that I'd have better luck, but it might be worth a shot.

There's only one thing guaranteed to cheer up Piper, and it's food. Hopefully, I can make it before the restaurant gets busy. The only thing I hate about the commute to

Dallas is the traffic. It's like people forget how to drive once the clock hits five. We all want to go home. Driving like an asshole isn't going to make things any better.

A horn blasts beside me as the person speeds up to get in front of me. I don't give them the satisfaction of a return honk. There's no point in road rage. Just a little further down the highway and you'll be home. It's the mantra I repeat to myself daily. Even if I am going to Piper's today, it's still home to me. I spend as much time there as I do at my house.

I watch the person who got in front of me, and I swear they'll end up causing a wreck. The car weaves in and out of lanes without regard to how close they're getting to others. It's not that serious.

Finally, I'm getting closer to Asheville and the traffic lightens up. I get over and take the ramp to town. If I was smart, I would have called in the order before I left work, but I didn't. It takes me a few moments to get downtown, and I park as close to Cavasos, the Mexican restaurant, as I can. Which is a few blocks away. Clearly, everyone else in town had the same idea because the line is to the door when I pull it open.

Piper is probably wondering where I am, but I don't want to text her because it'll ruin the surprise. Though, at this point, I don't know how much of a surprise it is. She knows good and well I always come with food. It's part of the best friend agreement. She does the same when she comes to my house. I don't even know how this whole tradition got started, but unless we go out to eat, the person visiting brings food. We both know it's supposed to be the other way around, but we don't care.

There's a small space available in the corner for me to

wait, and I lean against the wall trying not to knock off any of the decor. One of the waitstaff sees me and comes over to me.

"Do you want the usual?"

The fact he knows what I usually order is a sign we come here way too often. When the food is good, it's hard not to.

"Yep."

"Piper, too?"

"Yes, please." I take in the people in line in front of me. "I can wait my turn. It's not a big deal."

He shrugs and backs away from me. "You aren't eating in the restaurant. Why should you have to wait? I'll get the order in. By the time you make it to the stand, it should be ready for you."

"Thank you."

He has no idea how much time he's saved me. There's definitely no reason to let Piper know I'm running late now. She knows how traffic is. Next time, I'm definitely ordering ahead no matter where I stop for food.

The line moves forward at a snail's pace. I guess the folks dining in aren't in any rush to get out. More people are coming in behind me. I haven't even made it to the stand when the guy from earlier waves me over. That was quick.

I hand him my card to pay for the meals, and he hands me the bag. After a quick signature, I'm on my way to my car. At least I don't have to stop for booze. Piper always has wine on hand. There's no point in buying more.

One thing I love about it being summer is its still daylight as I pull into Piper's driveway at seven o'clock. The unfortunate thing…it's still hot as hell out here.

After putting the car into park, I grab the food and hurry to her front door. All I need is the cold air being inside promises me. Music is blasting through the house as I knock on the door. It's not the usual pop music she listens to either. Rock is reserved for bad days, and based on her text message earlier, today calls for it.

She doesn't hear me knocking, and I test the door knob to see if it's unlocked. Of course it is. No matter how many times I tell her she needs to lock it, she doesn't. In her eyes, she lives close enough to the winery and far enough from town for anyone to break in. I close the door and lock it behind me. If not, there's a likelihood any of her siblings will walk right in. It's not that I have anything against them, but tonight is about cheering up Piper, not bringing her down again.

I make my way through the foyer and make a short detour to the kitchen to set the food on the counter. When I enter the living room, I find exactly what I expect.

Piper is sprawled on the couch. A bottle of wine is open on the coffee table, but I don't see a glass. Okay, so she's taking the rejection harder than normal. Plus, she's always been a bit dramatic.

I grab the remote from the table and turn down the music before setting it back down. Piper doesn't move. She's not asleep. Instead, she's zoned out and lost in her thoughts. I hate the way her family makes her feel. She's just as much a part of Starlit Fields as them, and they don't give her a voice. At least, not unless it benefits them. And by them, I mean mostly Pierce. He'll be the boss when their dad retires.

I could lift her up, so I can sit down and hold her. It's probably better that I don't. Every time I console her, it rips a hole in my heart. Not just because of her family, but also because she's the person I'll never get to have as more than a friend. There are too many years of friendship to ruin it, and I don't want to lose her being a part of my life.

"Piper," I whisper. She doesn't answer, just continues to stare at the ceiling. "I brought food."

Those three little words are all it takes for her to acknowledge I'm here. She knows I came in. I just wanted to give her time to collect herself. She'll speak when she's ready. It's not often she doesn't have something to say over the years I've known her.

"What did you bring? Hopefully something that goes well with that." She points toward the bottle on the table.

"You'll have to get up and find out." I stand up and reach for her hand.

"Fine," she groans, but takes my hand. "Just say you hate me like the rest of my family."

"First off, I could never hate you." I lift her from the couch and lead her toward the kitchen. "Second of all, it's kind of mean to lump me in with your siblings when you're mad at them."

"I'm sorry. They are irritating, though. My presentation was amazing, but they wouldn't even take the chance. They are too scared of change. Parker said he agreed with my ideas after the meeting."

"Did he speak up with Pierce in the room?"

"No."

"Then his opinion doesn't matter."

She sees the bag on the counter and her face lights up. "You got Mexican food?"

"Yep, and it did exactly what I intended."

She lets go of my hand and moves to grab plates out of the cabinet. "What's that?"

"Make you happy."

She sets the plates down and throws her arms around me. "That is why I love you."

"I love you, too." As more than a friend, but I'll never tell her.

three

. . .

piper

GOOD GOD, why did I drink so much with Beau last night? It's been a while since I've had a hangover, but I don't remember it kicking my ass like this.

Thankfully, the office is mostly quiet. I can hear music playing from somewhere out front. It's not enough to really bug me, though. It might be light jazz? Parker decided it was a good idea to have some sort of music playing when people come in to buy their wine directly from us. He was right, but I'll never tell him that. Mostly because he doesn't have my back when it matters.

My head feels like there's someone banging on drums inside it. The knock on the office door doesn't help matters.

"Come in." Having to deal with people today is not something I want to do, but it's better than hearing the pounding on the door.

"Hey, Sister," Parker says as he walks in. "How ya doing this morning?"

"Please, stop yelling." I hold my hand up to stop him.

"I wasn't." He takes a seat in the chair across from the desk. "You look like hell."

"Gee, thanks." The office is a common area for everyone. I don't know why he felt the need to knock. Everybody usually walks in unannounced.

"Is it a migraine? I have some ibuprofen in my truck. I can grab it for you."

"No, it's not a migraine." I reach into my desk and pull out my bottle of medicine. "I've got some right here, thank you."

"Ah, so you took the meeting to heart?"

"What's that supposed to mean?"

"Well, if it's not a migraine or a regular headache, that means you went home and drank away your frustration."

He's not wrong, but I don't want him to know how much it affects me when they don't take me seriously.

"I may have drunk too much with Beau last night. No big deal."

"I see." He nods as if he knows something I don't. "Hope the hangover goes away."

"Did you need something?"

"Huh?" He's already standing and making his way toward the door.

"You came in here for a reason. Did you need something?"

He scratches the back of his head. It's one of his tells when he has bad news, or doesn't know how to say whatever he's thinking. He's done it since we were kids. I guess some things are never outgrown. It doesn't give me much hope they'll ever take me seriously.

"Yeah, Pierce said he needs to talk to you."

"He couldn't come to me himself?" It figures. He always sends someone else to do his bidding. I know he's technically the boss. But that doesn't mean ordering everyone around because you don't want to do it yourself.

"He's in the middle of unloading bottles. I offered." He didn't. Peter is the only one who offers to do anything without being asked. He's always trying to prove himself to our big brother. One day he'll realize no matter what he does…it'll never be enough. It's just sad it'll take so long for him to come to the conclusion.

"Give me a few and I'll go see what he wants."

He gives me a salute and walks out the door, closing it behind him. I really hate that everyone in the family, aside from Paula, bows down to Pierce's every whim. It's the only reason he continues to push everyone around.

I swear he's like the bully in school that continues to pick on you until you finally stand up for yourself. The only difference is when I do it, he makes it more of a point to ignore anything I have to say. It's infuriating.

A few minutes. That's all I need to get myself put together and face him. The last thing he needs to know is I'm nursing a hangover. I'll never hear the end of it. At least I didn't come to work still drunk like a few of my brothers have on occasion. And what did I do? I took up for them because that's what a good sibling does. At least, when it's not hurting anyone else.

I slip my shoes on before leaving the office. Honestly, being able to hang out without shoes at work is one of the perks of handling the social media. Though, it'll be nice if one day I'm able to turn one of these rooms into a studio for all of my ideas. It's not like all the rooms in this old house are being used. Most of them are blocked off to the public and are sitting empty. It's another idea I planned on launching, but I have a feeling it would go as well as the last meeting.

The walk from the main building to the production facility is a bit of a trek. My great grandpa wanted to be able to leave work at work. He didn't want the temptation of going back out there when he should be spending time with his family.

I still think it's pretty cool our main building was once their house. Rooms were added on as the family grew, and it's a nice touch of Starlit Fields history we could add into our branding story. Maybe if I bring that up to Pierce, he'll let me add it to the site. I can even find one of the photos of the house our parents have at their place. It makes for a great story and gives some insight into where our winery came from.

There are so many ideas bouncing around my head, and I worry they will never come to fruition because my brother simply doesn't care. Or, he doesn't care enough to make our company shine the way it could.

When I get to the production building, he's unloading bottles and setting them on a shelf. They still need our labels on them, but he always waits to do it. He doesn't want to make too many labels if we don't have enough wine to bottle it.

"Parker said you needed to see me?"

He looks up from the bottles in his hand. "Yeah. We need to update the website and I need you to take some photos of the new wine."

What is he talking about? I don't remember him saying anything about a new wine. Although, I also tuned him out during most of the meeting yesterday. He might be a little right when it comes to me acting childish. It's not that I do it on purpose. At least, not most of the time. Yesterday…I just couldn't be bothered to give a damn about what he had to say.

"Do we have any of the new wine bottled up?"

"Yes." He nods to the left. "We just need the usual stock picture and information about the wine.

"Okay." I fail to see why he had me come all the way out here for that. He could have brought me a bottle when he was done unloading. "Is there anything else?"

He doesn't say anything for a few minutes and keeps unloading bottles. He opens his mouth at the exact time I turn to leave. "Next time you have an idea, you need to come to me before you ambush everyone in the meeting. It was unprofessional to go behind my back like that."

Is he fucking serious right now? As if I haven't tried going to him with ideas in the past. He shot them down in private and I doubt he ever took them to Dad. This time at least it was in a public setting so the rest of the family could see I have some perspective when it comes to the company. They'll always see me as the person who does as she's told and doesn't do anything more than they ask.

Well, that changes now. I'm not going to let Pierce know because I don't think he deserves the heads up. No, I'll show up in ways that matter when it comes to the winery. Ones that will have proof and data behind it.

I know for a fact it's the only way I'll win our dad over. Even Pierce won't say no to a suggestion Dad makes. This time I'll gather what I need and go directly to him. Pierce isn't the boss of Starlit Fields yet. I'll take this time to remind him.

"Is there anything else you need?"

"No." He moves to the other shelf holding the filled bottles and grabs one. "You need this to take the photo for the website."

"Oh, yeah. Thanks." I grab the bottle from him and hurry out of the building. He has more audacity than anyone I've ever met. Even Parker, who's known to be over the top, would never talk down to anyone like that.

It never ceases to amaze me how we were all raised exactly the same, yet have come out so different from one another. Clearly, Pierce got hit with the asshole branch at some point in his life, and it shows every single day.

This time I'm taking the kill them with kindness approach. It's what he'll least expect. Who knows, maybe he'll appreciate the work I put in.

One of the perks of working for the family, and handling minimal tasks, is I get to leave early if everything is done.

My phone dings with a message as soon as I get home.

BEAU

Wanna hang out tonight?

PIPER

Sorry, I have a date. Thanks for last night by the way.

BEAU

Oh cool, hope it goes well.

The fact he's wishing me luck speaks volumes of my dating life. Every single date I've been on the past few months has been disastrous. None of them meet the expectations I've set for myself. I don't know if it's because my parents taught me to have high standards, or if it's because none of them will ever replace Beau.

I don't really have time to worry about that right now, though. I need to get ready for tonight.

PIPER

Thanks. I'll share my location when I get to the restaurant. You know in case the guy tries to kidnap me.

BEAU

I seriously doubt that would happen. But sounds good.

He says that every time I tell him I'm sharing my location. It's a safeguard that makes me feel more comfortable going places without him. I mean, it would be weird to show up to a date with my best friend. The one time I suggested it, Beau looked at me like I'd lost my mind.

He's the one person who has always made me feel safe. I've been in love with him since the day he helped me carry my flowers home in middle school. Too bad I'll never do anything to jeopardize our friendship. He's too important to me. It's why I keep going on these dates. Maybe one of these guys will make me forget the feelings I've always harbored for Beau.

Eventually one of these guys will knock my socks off, right? At least once I should be able to hit the dating jackpot. I'm not holding my breath, though. For whatever reason, I tend to attract people who are self-involved, only want to get free booze, or think they're getting in my pants right after the date. Sorry, that's not happening. Nothing against folks who live more freely than me, but I need to know sex isn't all they're after.

My phone dings again, but this time it's the alarm. A not so gentle reminder I need to leave sooner than later to avoid hitting traffic.

I rush to my room and quickly change. A glance in the mirror shows my hair and makeup are still perfect from this morning. It takes me a few seconds to share my location with Beau before grabbing my clutch and hauling ass out the front door. Being late isn't the first impression I want to give this guy.

four

. . .

beau

IT'S TAKING everything in me not to constantly check Piper's location. I wasn't playing when I said I didn't think anyone would try to abduct her. But it's for my own peace of mind, too. You can't trust people these days, and she has a penchant for choosing douchebags to go on dates with.

If only she saw me as a viable dating option. She doesn't realize how happy I could make her. I won't bring it up, though. I can't. Not at the risk of losing her forever. For now, I'll stick to being the person she comes to when she needs me. It's what I've done for over a decade, and what I'll continue doing.

My phone vibrates in my hand and it scares the shit out of me. I glance at the message.

PIPER

You home?

BEAU

Yeah. What's up?

PIPER

I'm coming over.

Okay. I wasn't expecting her to need me quite so soon. Preparations probably need to be made. If she's leaving her date this early it didn't go well at all.

I grab my keys from the counter and head out the door. My house isn't as well stocked as hers. But I know she'll want her favorite wine and maybe some cupcakes. There's no point in getting dinner for the both of us since I'm sure she's already eaten. Or, maybe she didn't. I've got food in the fridge I can cook if she's hungry.

My shopping trip takes me twenty minutes and I'm unloading the bags when the door opens. She almost beat me here. Was she speeding the entire way? I glance at the clock on the stove. No wonder she got here so fast. The traffic should be non-existent by now.

"You talk about me not locking my door. I literally just walked right in, and I was prepared." She jangles her keys in her hand. Both of us have a key to each other's house. It makes it easier for both of us. Not that she ever locks her damn door.

"To be fair, I just got home."

"Oh." She sets her keys on the counter and walks into the kitchen. "Did I interrupt whatever plans you had?"

"Nope." I shake my head and lift the items I bought moments ago. "I was getting things we needed."

She leans over and kisses me on the cheek. They grow warm and I hope like hell she can't see me blushing. That is exactly what I don't need to happen.

"You are the best because we're going to need it."

"That bad, huh?"

She grabs the bottle of wine and digs around in the drawer for the corkscrew. "Bad doesn't even begin to describe the shit show that took place."

Since she's taking care of the wine. I grab a couple of glasses and the cupcakes, following her into the living room. "Well, you can rant to me about it."

"If only it was just the date."

"What do you mean?"

"Pierce threw some passive aggressive comments toward me at work. Basically, do what I'm told and nothing more."

"That's fucked up. Didn't he say his piece in the meeting?"

"I thought so." She sighs and pours the wine into our glasses. "Apparently, he needed to take one more jab to drive the point home."

"I'm sorry, Piper. That really sucks." I take a drink from my glass. "Is there anything I can do to help? I mean, changing their minds will be difficult, but it's worth a shot."

"Actually…I have an idea." She pulls her phone out of her pocket and opens one of her social media pages. "What if I go live right now? It's not like they'd even know since most of them rarely get on socials."

"How are you going to do that without any product to showcase? Besides, aren't there rules about showing off booze?"

"We have a bottle right here." She lifts the wine bottle off the table. "It can be like a Q&A type of thing."

"And what happens when Pierce finds out? Asheville

is a small town. Word will get back to him sooner than later."

I hate being the one to bring her back down to reality. We've spent so much time dreaming up big things for Starlit Fields. But I don't want her to get any more backlash from her big brother than she's already received.

"It'll be too late." She shrugs, but she doesn't immediately hit the button that will take her live. "Actually, this is something we should ease into. Scoot closer to me."

She knows I'll always do what she says. Does it make me a pushover? Maybe. But she's my reason for breathing, whether or not she knows it.

"What are we doing?" She implied seconds ago we weren't going live. It's not a bad idea, but I don't need her brother busting down my door for letting her do it. They know what the inside of my house looks like should someone let him know she's online. Though, the only person I can see being that in tune with the Starlit Fields social media is Parker. I doubt he'd tell on her. At least, not intentionally.

"Say cheese." A snap fills the quiet in the room before I have a chance to do anything. She glances at her phone and frowns. "That's horrible. Let's take another one."

"It wouldn't have been if you'd given me more than two seconds notice." I laugh and lean in. She snaps another picture. "You realize you're supposed to countdown, right?"

"Where's the fun in that? People love candid moments."

She's not wrong. We've gotten so much data from social media users saying they want slice of life types of posts. Now, it's time to see what she's going to do with it.

"That's kind of impossible when you tell me you're taking a picture."

She taps at the keyboard on her phone and grins as she sets it down on the table. "There."

"What did you do?"

"I posted a story with a questions box. We're doing an impromptu ask me anything."

I've seen the amount of followers Starlit Fields has. I'm not sure anything is going to come of this. If it was planned…maybe. But just posting this late in the evening with no warning, it may be a bit more difficult.

"That's good." How do I break this down to her simply? "Even if nobody asks a question, we can still hang out and finish this wine. Speaking of, you never got into the details of the date from hell."

"You really know how to bring the mood down, don't you?"

"I'm just curious what happened. You never leave a date as early as you did today."

There's a high probability he was an asshole. Most of the guys she goes on dates with are. If only I wasn't safely tucked away in the friend category. I put myself there the day I met her. Dumb move on my part, but worth it to have her in my life at all.

"I didn't even make it to the meal." She groans and takes another drink of her wine. "It was so bad. He was already at the table when I got there. I don't understand how you drive in that traffic every day. I'll take these backroads any day of the week."

"Stop trying to change the subject." Deflection is her superpower after spending years trying to get her siblings to not pick on her because she's the baby.

"Fine." She pouts. "Anyway, I get there and he's talking to a woman. I think, cool, it's probably someone coming to take the order. She walks off right before I get to the table. We exchange introductions as soon as I sit down. Thank God his picture was accurate. You wouldn't believe how many people upload ones that aren't. So, we're sitting down and picking up where we left off in our chat. Some other woman, who is in fact part of the waitstaff, comes to take our order. I get a drink and an appetizer, but in the process, I see him slip this woman his number."

"Excuse me, what?" That's bold. I could never imagine trying to talk to someone else when I'm on a date. Much less in front of them.

"I know!" She pours more wine into her glass. Honestly, I wouldn't blame her if she drank straight from the bottle. "When I said something about it, he tried to wave it away as if I didn't see what just happened. I told him I wouldn't be gaslit and he could take this date and shove it."

"At least you found out early on." Now I know she's drinking on an empty stomach, and that's never a good thing. "I'm going to order us something from Out of the Ashes and have it delivered."

"You don't have to do that." She reaches for my phone. "That means you'll have gotten dinner two nights in a row."

"It's fine. You've been through enough bullshit this week. Let me do this for you."

"Okay." She knows there's no use in arguing. It's not like I have to ask what she wants. She finds something she likes and eats it for eternity rather than branching out. "Why can't any of my dates turn out decent? It's like I'm a jerk magnet. As much as my brothers annoy the shit out of me, they taught me not to be gaslit by anyone. Well, except Pierce. He does a pretty good job of that."

"I'm just glad you didn't take any of that dude's shit." Maybe someday she'll realize there could be something between us. I would treat her like a queen. Even if that day never comes, I'll be fine. "You'll find someone who matches your energy. You have to be patient. And the food will be here in about twenty minutes."

"Seriously, thank you for everything you do for me."

"I've got your back. Always have and always will."

"That is why you're the best."

A few moments pass by and we enjoy the companionable silence. This is how easy it should be. It's not like this all the time between us. We've fought and not talked to each other for short periods of time. But the way we can be ourselves in each other's company is unmatched.

Her phone lights up and she squeals as she picks it up.

"What happened?" I don't remember the last time I've seen her excited like this.

"There are so many responses to the story I posted." She turns toward me with a devious grin.

"What are you about to do?"

"Something my brother will absolutely hate, but there are so many comments." I open my mouth to argue about why it's not a good idea, but she waves her hands in the air. "Don't worry, I'm not going live. But I am going to do video responses."

"Okay…" I'm not sure what that has to do with me. But this is definitely better than her going live. The last thing she needs is one of her siblings to join in the conversation and possibly ruin the experience for her.

"And you're going to be in them with me."

"Why do I need to be in the videos with you?"

"Because you're my emotional support human. And everyone likes a little eye candy."

Her cheeks flush as she says it. At least I know she finds me attractive outside of being my friend.

"Fine." I make it sound like I don't want to do it, but I'm glad she considers me her safe space. And…I would do anything for her.

She taps on the first question. "Are you ready?"

I nod in response, and she hits record. As soon as I see the question, I shake my head.

Who is the cutie next to you?

She laughs, but responds. "This is my best friend, Beau. I've known him forever, and we've been through thick and thin together."

I give a small wave. Honestly, I didn't think I would be the topic of a question, but I'll play along. For her.

Next question. What is your favorite wine?

Piper holds up her glass and hits the record button. "Our sangria is my absolute favorite. It's also one requested by customers at our winery. If you want to try it out, you can come down to Starlit Fields or visit Out of the Ashes. They keep bottles in stock for their patrons."

We spend about thirty minutes answering questions. Well, not so much me. I'm merely there for support, and to get the food. It showed up mid answer and she explained what I was doing while still keeping the focus on the wine. Maybe Out of the Ashes will get more business with her shout outs.

Piper was right when she said fans of the winery want to hear from them. I think it adds a personal touch to the business. If the customers get to know you, they're more likely to buy from you. Now we need her brother to realize it.

Piper finally gets to the last question and sets her phone down on the table. "That was epic."

"You did amazing." It's not a lie. She's a natural on camera and I wish her family could see it. She needs to be the social media face for the winery.

Without realizing what's happening, she leans over and her lips crash into mine. Holy shit. Piper Summers is kissing me in a more than friendly way.

five

. . .

piper

IT TAKES me at least a minute to realize what I've done. Of course, I've probably ruined our friendship. I immediately pull back and bury my face in my hands.

"Oh my God. I'm so sorry." Beau reaches for me and I scoot away from him. "I shouldn't have done that."

"Piper, it's fine." His voice is calm. That's a good sign. Doesn't mean I don't feel like I overstepped a boundary.

His hands circle my wrists as he tries to pull my hands from my face. Too bad it's not happening. There's no way I'm letting him see the embarrassment I feel right this second. If the ground opens up and swallows me whole, I'll be completely fine with it.

I turn in the other direction planning my escape. In the years we've been friends, Beau has seen me do a lot of dumb things, but this takes the cake. There's no excuse for me kissing him. Especially when I don't even know how he feels about me.

I move to get off the couch, but Beau's voice stops me.

"Damn it, Piper, would you look at me?"

It's not the words that make me turn toward him. It's the frustration in his voice. I've never shut him out like this. He didn't even do anything wrong. It was me.

The pain in his eyes breaks my heart. It shouldn't since I'm the one who put it there.

"I don't know what came over me, Beau. I really am sorry."

He grabs my hand and laces his fingers through mine. An action we've done hundreds of times since we were teens, but this time it feels...different. Or, maybe it's just me.

"If you think one kiss is going to make me question our friendship, you don't know me at all."

"That's not what I think." It's partially true. Do I think I screwed things up between us? Yes. But I know that's fixable over time.

"Why were you trying to run away?" He gives my hand a squeeze. "You don't run unless you're scared. Hell, even then, I've never seen you run."

"Embarrassment." I study the fabric of my jeans. "I kissed my best friend. Without your consent I might add. I was too caught up in the excitement and reacted."

"It wasn't a bad kiss. If that makes you feel better."

He really thinks that will make me feel better? It doesn't. He's basically saying the kiss was okay. Talk about a punch to the ego. Never in my life has anyone said kissing me was not bad.

"You sure know how to make a gal feel better."

"I didn't mean it like that." This time he studies his

pants and pulls his hand free from mine. Things are definitely weird now.

"What did you mean, then?" There isn't much he could say that would make me feel any better about the situation I've put us in.

"All I'm saying is I wasn't opposed to the kiss." His eyes meet mine and they are no longer full of sadness. Is that hope? "And I wouldn't be if you did it again."

Whoa…what? I must not have heard that right. He wouldn't be opposed to kissing again? Not the words I was expecting to hear. Too bad it's not a good idea.

"W-we probably shouldn't." I'm back to staring at the floor. It's too much to look at him and see the possible disappointment. Even if I am flattered, he thinks I'm a good kisser. "We're both caught up in the moment. It doesn't mean anything."

Lie. Probably the biggest one I've ever told myself. The kiss itself may not have been long and passionate, but it was perfect. He kissed me back, though.

"Piper, I know you're my best friend and know me better than anyone else, but I'm gonna need you to not tell me how I feel." He sighs, and even though I'm not looking at him, I know he's running his hand through his hair. It's what he does when he's frustrated and trying to find the right words. "The kiss took me by surprise, but I'm not mad it happened. I've wanted it too, for so long."

"What do you mean?" I wanted to ask how long, but I'm not sure I want the answer to that.

"I mean, I think we're both at an age where we can explore what would happen between us as more than friends."

He's not wrong in that aspect, but what if it ruins

everything between us. I cannot lose him as my best friend. He's the only person who completely understands me. Not even my siblings can say that.

Now, I do look at him. I want to see his reaction to what I'm about to say.

"I think we should keep things on the friend level. I love you, Beau, but I don't want anything to change for us. You are the one constant in my life, and I can't lose that. Who else would I turn to when shit hits the fan at the winery? And who would you seek out when your annoying coworker won't stop breathing over you. If we were to see how we do as a couple, and things go south, we lose each other completely. I can't live with that."

Shockingly, he doesn't look upset. More resigned, like he knew what I was going to say. I may try new things when it comes to my job, but I can't risk that with him.

"I get it." He nods and leans back against the cushion. I thought he would put up a fight. "But…when you're ready to take that leap, I'll be here."

"How do you know I'll ever reach that point?"

"Who knows you better than anyone? Me. That kiss meant something." He points to my mouth. "Whether you want to admit it or not. And I'm good at waiting."

Well, he's becoming awfully cocky. I'm not sure how I feel about that. "Whatever you say. Let's finish eating and watch a movie."

"I know." He taps his finger to his forehead. Ugh, he can be so annoying. "What do you want to watch?"

The way he can flip from serious conversation to fun has always astounded me. I'll be replaying this entire conversation for days and overthinking it because that's what I do. I may have a go-getter attitude on the outside, but I always second guess what I do.

"It doesn't matter to me. Pick something we haven't seen before."

He picks a movie I've never heard of and we settle into the movie. I don't even know what genre it is, but I guess we're about to find out.

This feels comfortable. Him beside me on his sofa watching a movie. We spent so many of our nights in high school just like this. Neither one of us could be bothered to go out and party with the rest of our classmates. We didn't need to. We had each other. If I take things further than friendship with him, we could lose nights like tonight. I know I've made the right decision. At least, I hope I did.

Parker's truck is sitting in my driveway when I pull in. This can't be good. The evening already started off rocky, even if Beau made it fine by the end of the night.

He walked me to my car like he normally does and waited until I left the driveway to go back inside. It felt the same and different. Like there was a charge in the air. I'm chalking it up to my impromptu kiss. That's the only explanation. And the fact he admitted he has feelings for me. I can't act on my own though. Anytime I try to take on something big lately, it's blown up in my face and I can't have it happen with him.

My brother is clearly here for a reason, and I need to push away any thoughts about Beau. I park my car and step out after turning it off. "How did you know I was on my way home?"

"We have that tracking app. I saw you were leaving Beau's and figured I'd meet you here." He grins to hide whatever it is that has him concerned.

"So, you were stalking me? Great."

"I wouldn't call it stalking. You're my sister, I had to make sure you were safe after your date."

"Yeah, well that went nowhere." I wave away the questions he's opening his mouth to ask. "Is there a reason you're here right now?"

He scratches the back of his neck. "Yes?"

"Sounds like you don't know. Clearly this could have been a text or waited until tomorrow."

"It could, but I wanted to warn you before you got into work. Pierce isn't happy."

"Still could have been a text." I grumble as I push past him and unlock my door. "What does he have stuck up his butt now?"

Parker follows me inside and closes the door behind us. "The Instagram stories."

Those three words stop me in my tracks. I thought for sure I'd have more time for him to find out. He's not chronically online like some of us. It's also why he doesn't know what's trending when it comes to growing businesses.

"How did he find out about those? I literally just did them."

He moves past me and heads straight to the sofa. "I'll give you two guesses, but you'll only need one."

He sits down, waiting for me to join him. Why are my brothers so damn intrusive? I drop my bag on the counter and head toward the fridge. I'll need a drink to deal with this mess.

"How did Peter even know?" I grab the two beers and head toward my brother. "I didn't even realize he had any social media accounts."

Parker shrugs and takes the beer I hold out for him. "I didn't either. Apparently, he set one up ages ago because his friends talked him into it. That's beside the point. He set up notifications for when the Starlit Fields account shares posts. He saw them and snitched to Pierce."

"One of these days he'll have to grow a spine and stop doing what others tell him he should."

The beer is cold against my mouth as I take a sip. I'd much rather be here with Beau. Hell, maybe if I'd stayed over there, I could have prolonged this encounter.

"I doubt that will happen. Not until it's something he really wants, anyway."

"Kissing Pierce's ass isn't going to make him any nicer toward him. I hope he knows that as he sells out his siblings one by one."

Maybe Paula was the smart one and got out when she could. She doesn't have to deal with any of this bullshit with our older brother. I'm shocked he didn't call to yell at me. I guess he's waiting until I see him in person.

"I don't think he cares." He takes a long swig of his beer. "What were you doing at Beau's? I thought you had a date."

"Are there no secrets in this family?" I throw my hands in the air.

"You know the answer to that question." He laughs at my reaction. He's right, but damn. There are some things I would rather not everyone know. "I'm guessing it didn't go well."

"Considering he was trying to pick up future dates while I was at the table…absolutely not."

"That's gross. I don't even have the audacity to do that. How did Beau like being a part of the stories?"

I can feel my cheeks warm at the sound of his name. Hopefully, my brother doesn't notice.

"He was a good sport about it."

"Of course he was. You have the poor guy wrapped around your finger."

"What's that supposed to mean?"

"If I have to explain it, you aren't ready to hear it."

It's not like Parker to be evasive like this. He has to know something I don't. Too bad I made my decision and don't want to know his thoughts.

"I kissed him." I don't know why I blurt it out, but I need to confide in someone.

"Whoa, what?" He shouts. Thank God I live pretty far away from the rest of the family, otherwise they may have heard his shout. He waves his hands in front of him. "Actually, never mind. I don't need to know about your sex life."

"Oh my God, Parker," I groan. "We didn't have sex. It was a kiss. I don't even know why I did it. The stories went great and it was a gut reaction."

"Maybe you should follow your gut more often." He shrugs and looks away.

"Pfft. As if I'd take any advice from you." I shake my head. "I followed my gut in the meeting and that didn't turn out well. Besides, it's not like I had your support."

"The support shouldn't matter, Little Sister. You should follow your heart."

"Nope." Doing that works for other people…not me. "I

don't want to screw things up with our friendship. It's the one thing I won't risk."

He finishes his beer and sets it on the coffee table. "I can't make you do anything, but think about it. Also, be prepared for the wrath of Pierce. I'm heading out."

"Take your bottle to the trash can. I'm not your maid."

"Yes, ma'am." He waves and grabs the bottle.

I really need for my family to butt out of my life unless I ask them for advice. Or, to you know, support me. The last thing I want from them is dating advice.

six

. . .

beau

ALL I'VE BEEN able to think about is Piper's lips on mine. I never in a million years thought it would happen. At least, not without me instigating it. She's wrong, though. We weren't caught up in the moment. Even if it took me by surprise, it felt right. Like something we should have been doing for years.

It's been a few days since she was at my house. While it's normal, it's also not. She hasn't texted me as much and I know she's avoiding me. She can lie and say she isn't, but I know her better than anyone else.

Too bad I have to be at work and can't confront her about it. I gave her the weekend to deal with what she was feeling. The only thing fueling me is hope she'll come to her senses and see how well we could work together. Not in the way she's expecting with the winery, but me and her. Us against the world the way we've always been…but with kissing and stuff.

I'll wait, though. I have been for years. A little longer won't hurt. The fact she kissed me means she does feel more for me. She only has to stop lying to herself.

My phone dings with a text. Reaching into my pocket, I pull it out. As soon as I see the name, the urge to shove it in my pocket takes over, even though I know I need to answer it. He'll keep blowing up my phone until I respond. He's persistent like that. Always has been and always will be.

PIERCE

We need to talk.

BEAU

Why? I don't remember doing anything wrong.

There's a rock in the pit of my stomach because I know what this is about. Honestly, I'm shocked it's taken him this long to reach out to me.

PIERCE

You didn't try to stop Piper from making those candid posts on social media?

For fuck's sake. If we keep texting this conversation could go on all day. Talking to Piper's big brother is the last thing I want to do, but I guess I have to. It's the only way he'll leave me alone. Putting it off will only make things worse.

At this point in life, I'm used to being dragged into Summers' family drama. But he doesn't know what he's up against if he thinks I'm going to abandon my best friend. There's nothing in this world that can make me turn my back on her. Including if she decides she really doesn't have feelings for me.

Instead of replying, I click his number and wait. It rings three times before he answers. It's a little long since I know for a fact he has his phone in his hand. My eyes roam around the office to make sure nobody is around.

Should I be making this call in the office? Absolutely not. It's worth whatever reprimand I may get.

"Hello?" He grunts. Oh great, I get to deal with annoyed Pierce. Better for me to catch his ire than Piper, though.

I don't bother with pleasantries. He didn't when he sent the text message, and doesn't deserve it from me. Especially when I have an idea of how this call will go.

"What exactly are you insinuating I did?" Better to be the one confronting him than the other way around.

"You let Piper make all those posts on social media. She was at your house. You could have easily said you didn't want to do it."

How the hell is he going to dictate what I do in my house? That's the thing with Pierce, though. He thinks he can steamroll over anyone he wants. Too bad life doesn't work that way. One day someone is going to push back and won't be nice about it. I actually hope I'm around to see it happen.

"Her making those short posts was better than her initial plan."

"What do you mean?"

"I mean, she was going to go live. I talked her out of that." I take a second to gather my thoughts. He needs to realize this was the better option, and the more controlled one. But it won't stop me from giving my two cents. "If you would give her some creative space on the socials, she wouldn't feel the need to go behind your back and do it."

"That's beside the point. I gave her a template to post. She strayed from that." According to him, whatever he says goes. He doesn't care about anyone else's input. My eyes roam the office to make sure I'm not getting anyone's attention.

"Did you know she consulted me about marketing tactics?"

He's silent on the other end. The words were out of my mouth before I realize it. Who knows if she mentioned it in the presentation. If he didn't know, it's too late now.

"No. Why would she? It's not her job."

Well, that answered the question about him knowing. Paul is making a huge mistake letting Pierce make all the decisions with Starlit Fields. It's this closeminded thinking that's going to tank the company.

"Because she sees a bigger future for the winery. Her presentation laid it all out. Those were the points we talked about. She also had me come up with a scaled down marketing plan in case you turned it down."

"Because we don't know if what she's planning will work."

"You'll never know unless you try."

"I've made my decision. You are Piper's voice of reason. Make sure she doesn't go behind my back again."

Why does he think he can order me around? Never in the years I've known him has he pulled this crap. He's always treated me like an annoying brother and acted like I wasn't there. But I just put myself on his radar when it comes to the winery. I don't understand why he thinks he has any sway over me.

"And if I don't? I can't control her every action, and I don't want to."

Silence fills the air and I wonder if he's hung up. I pull the phone away from my ear and check the screen. The call is still open. Whatever comes out of his mouth next won't be good.

"If you don't, I'll find someone to handle the socials and office the way I believe it should be done."

Wait…he can't be saying what I think he is. Does he mean he'll fire her?

Before I can argue he hangs up. He always has to have the last word. I've known what Piper has gone through, but this is the first time I can honestly imagine what it feels like to be in her shoes.

The urge to call him back is overwhelming. It'll make things worse, and the last thing I want is for him to take it out on Piper.

How the hell am I supposed to be supportive of what she wants to do when it comes to the winery while also making sure she doesn't lose her job. She can't know about what he just told me. At least, not yet.

I set my phone on my desk and get back to work. These clients won't take care of themselves. Too bad my concentration is now blown to bits.

My hand inches toward my phone again. Not to call Pierce, but to warn Piper her brother is in a mood and to steer clear of him. Her well-being is all I care about.

"Beau." Cole appears at the side of my desk. I didn't even see him walk up, and I push my phone to the side. The last thing I need is for him to tattle on me for being on the phone. He's a nice guy, but he'll do anything to get a leg up in the company.

"Yeah?" Dealing with him isn't on my agenda today. Not after talking to Pierce.

"The boss wants to see you." He nods toward the office on the other side of the room. "He said you can finish up what you're working on first."

"Thanks." I put the finishing touches on this proposal and send it off to the client. Apparently today is going to be a doozy between Pierce and my boss. There are too many thoughts bouncing around in my head and talking to my boss will only add to the noise.

Deep breath in and out. Whatever Mr. Gardner has to say can't be bad. I'm a model employee aside from that quick conversation with Pierce. I guess it's time to find out what he wants from me. Hopefully it's not to add more to my work load.

My steps are slow and measured across the room. The longer I take to get to his office, the longer I can put off this impromptu meeting.

"Close the door." Mr. Gardner says as I approach his office. This isn't a good sign.

"What can I do for you, Sir?" I take a seat in one of the uncomfortable chairs across from him. You'd think he'd have better ones with the high caliber clients he meets. Maybe I'll suggest it to him assuming he's not firing me. If clients are comfortable, they are more likely to agree to any plans he offers.

He leans back in his chair and clasps his hands over his chest. It looks uncomfortable, and I don't know why older men do it. Maybe he thinks it makes him look more important? It doesn't. He looks like he's one step away from stuffing his hands under his armpits.

"Cole told me you were putting together two proposals for a potential client." Of course he did.

"Well, it was more of a favor to a friend. They're a small business and don't have the funds to be an actual client." At least, I don't think they do.

"I'd like to take a look at them."

"Why?" The word is out of my mouth before I can reel it back in. Questioning your boss on something you did for a nonpaying client probably isn't a good idea.

Now he leans forward. Having the attention of my boss is weird. I'm a fly below the radar type of guy. I come in, do my job, then go home. None of this other stuff is needed. Damn Cole for opening his big mouth.

"If both plans are solid, I'd like you to test them both. If we can make it work for an up and coming small business, it's possible we can garner the same results for our larger clients. But on a bigger scale."

"They can't afford both marketing plans. At least not the one on one." I'm going to murder Cole.

"I understand that. Is this something you'd be helping you friend with on a personal level without company time?"

Absolutely. I've always done what I can to help Starlit Fields. "Yes. That was my initial plan. I just wanted to run some numbers up here to give them a ballpark figure."

Where is he going with this?

"Then do whatever you were going to do. If one of them proves to be successful, I'd like you to let me know. There may be a promotion in it for you."

This isn't at all what I was expecting. More money would be great, but at what cost.

"I like working with small businesses, Mr. Gardner. I'm not sure I'd want to be promoted to the larger clients."

"Then show me how you can do it on a budget." He reaches for his phone, an indication the conversation is over. "Maybe we can work something out."

"Okay." I'm almost certain Cole was trying to get me in trouble. Too bad it seems to have backfired on him.

"Keep me updated." His attention is one hundred percent on his phone now.

"I will." Without another word I stand and walk out of the office, closing the door behind me. Now I have to keep Piper from doing anything on socials while also showing my boss the marketing plans can work. What in the world did I just get myself into?

seven

. . .

piper

PINS AND NEEDLES. That's what I've been sitting on for days. Every time I bump into my eldest brother, I ready myself for a confrontation. Parker said he was pissed, but he hasn't said anything to me.

Still, I creep around every corner to make sure he isn't in the area. It's kind of sad I have to do that while at work with my own family, but I don't want the confrontation. The fight that would come about isn't worth it. At least, not right now.

The desk is covered with various papers and I have to sort through them before I can get any work done. We really need two desks in this room. One for me and one for everyone to put their crap on.

A piece of paper slips from the pile. Is that a parking ticket? These fools should know the company isn't paying for those. I scan the name for who it might belong to.

Philip. Of course it is. He thinks because he's one of

the middle kids nobody will notice when he does crap like this. When Mom took care of all the admin stuff, she probably let it slide. Well, guess what, buddy. I'm not mom.

Maybe I would have swept it under the rug if he had spoken up during the meeting last week, but I'm feeling particularly petty today. He'll find a nice surprise in his truck when he gets off work.

Now that all the paperwork is sorted and where it's supposed to be, I can get to work on the orders. The queue is full. I don't remember the last time we had this many orders outside of the ones we do for a few bars in the area. They aren't all to one place either.

It looks like people have found us. This is a reason I put a maximum number of orders we can take at a time. Though I never thought we'd actually get this many at once. Maybe my stories did what they were supposed to and brought in business. I haven't been tracking it, so I can't be sure. It could also be because parents need a reprieve from their busy schedules now that school is back in session.

Actually, the latter makes sense. The stories were days ago. If we were going to see a bump in sales it would have happened then. Maybe Pierce is right. My time may not be better spent finding new ways to engage with our audience. I refuse to tell him that. The last thing I want to hear is I told you so.

"Hey, sister." Philip pokes his head into the office. "Did you get that thing I put on your desk?"

Funny how he doesn't mention it by name. "That depends. What exactly are you looking for?"

The thing in question is sitting to the left of my

keyboard. I guess I won't have to put it in his truck after all.

"It's a piece of paper about this big." He holds his hands up in the air showing a small rectangle. "It needs to be taken care of soon."

"Oh," I pick up the ticket. "You mean this?"

"Yes!" He comes further into the office. "Can you get that paid today?"

"Did Pierce sign off on it?"

"W-what?" Sweat beads on his forehead. It could be from being outside, or the realization he'll have to go to our big brother. "Dad never signed off on them."

"How many tickets have you gotten, Philip?"

"A few." He shrugs his shoulder and sits in the chair across from the desk. "Mom always paid them so I never had to worry about it."

"Maybe you should slow down." I glance down at the ticket in question. "And maybe not park in front of a fire hydrant."

"I wasn't even parked that long," he groans. "I had to run into the hardware store to get some screws. It was like two minutes."

"Long enough for an officer to see it and give you a ticket." I hand it over to him. "If you can get Pierce to sign off on it, I'll get it paid. You know how he's been with getting expenses approved."

There is definitely fear in his eyes. He knows good and well our brother would never. If anything, he'd rip him a new one for having so many. If I paid it without his signature, it'd be my ass on the line. I'm already on his list of people he's annoyed with. There's no way in hell I'm making that worse.

"Fine." He stands and pulls his phone out of his pocket. He's definitely paying it himself. Even he's scared to approach our big brother. I don't blame him one bit. He stops before leaving the office. "Are you leaving early today?"

"Why would I?" There's nothing on my calendar. I double check to be sure.

"There are some wild storms that are supposed to come in. I think Pierce is going to call it an early day for everyone."

"It's not like we live far from the winery." My grand-parents had a massive plot of land and each of us has a piece. Even Paula, though she refuses to build a house on it. That may change now that she's with Tristan. "All of us can get to our houses in like five minutes or less."

"Whatever it is has him worried." He shrugs his shoulders. "Do you want me to check with him?"

"No," I shake my head. "I'll ask him. I need to take him all these orders anyway."

"Okay. Let me know what he says."

I nod and he walks out the door. It only takes a couple of minutes to print the orders, and before long I'm heading into the metal building that stores our bottles of wine.

"Here are the orders for today."

Pierce glances over at me and notices the stack in my hand. "That looks like a lot."

"It is. I don't know what happened but these were all in the system when I logged in this morning." I hand them over to him. "Oh, and Philip mentioned something about leaving early today."

"I guess he wanted you to pay for the ticket I saw on the desk yesterday while he was there." There's nothing my brother doesn't notice. Of course, he already knew about it.

"Yep. I told him you had to sign off on it. He took it and I guess he's paying for it himself."

"As he should." Pierce pulls out his phone and taps on the screen a few times before showing me the radar. "But yeah, we're probably heading out early. I don't want any of us to get stuck in the storm. They're calling for tornadoes."

That's the last thing I want to hear. "I should probably pull all my candles out when I get home just in case we lose power. Are the backup generators ready to go here?"

"Yeah. I'll probably stay here tonight in case anything goes wrong. Do you want to help me get these orders packed up so we can get them sent out before it hits?"

Not really. Packing orders means I'll be stuck with my least favorite family member. But he's right. We need to get these orders out unless we want angry customers. "Sure."

I cross my fingers, hoping he doesn't say anything else. Storms make me uneasy as it is, and the last thing I want to do is get into another argument with my brother.

The sky is dark and the winds are already picking up when I pull into my driveway. We managed to get all the orders shipped out and I'm grateful Pierce let us go home early. I need to mentally prepare for tonight.

As soon as I'm inside, I grab my phone out of my bag. I may be avoiding him a bit lately, but I need to make sure he's aware of what the weather is doing.

It only takes a few minutes for a response to pop up.

Now, I need to find all my candles. I haven't been home as much and haven't had them burning like I usually do.

It doesn't take me long to go through all the rooms and gather as many candles as possible onto the coffee table. The lighter is sitting to the side of them should I need them. I hope the power doesn't go out. Living in the middle of nowhere with neighbors at least a mile apart, it can get very dark without any sort of light source. I may or may not have grown out of my fear of the dark.

A few moments later, I pull the mega bright flashlight my grandpa gave me out from under the sink. Between this and the candles, I should be set. A small part of me wishes I would have gone to one of my brothers' houses for the night. But I'm still annoyed with them. Pride will be the death of me, I swear.

Food is next on the agenda and I preheat the oven to cook a frozen pizza. It's a comfort food, and I don't have to worry about it going to waste. It's also quick and doesn't dirty many dishes. A double win for me.

The leaves on the trees outside my kitchen window are swaying in the wind. I can hear them brushing against each other, and the house, and I know it's going to be a bad storm. After sliding the pizza into the oven, I get any other supplies I might need.

The blanket from the foot of my bed, my pillow, and a stuffed animal Beau won for me at one of Asheville's festivals. I've had it since high school, and while it may be well loved, it never strays far from me when I sleep. A small flashlight from my nightstand gets moved to the bathroom for a light source since it's at the end of the hall.

Ding. My dinner is done and I rush to pull the pizza out of the oven and slide it on a plate. Once it's sliced the way I like it, I grab it and a bottle of water before heading to my sofa.

With my phone plugged in and the TV playing one of my favorite romcoms, I dig in. The only thing that would make tonight less stressful is Beau sitting beside me and making fun of me for taking so many precautions. It's all in good fun and I miss it.

No, Piper. You need to stop focusing on Beau. My intrusive thoughts are right. The only way to keep thoughts of kissing my best friend at bay is to look for a date. I grab my phone and open one of the dating apps. The first guy to pop up is one I've been on a date with before. I really need to remember to block the duds. He was nice enough. We didn't really have any chemistry, though.

As I'm swiping through, a crash of thunder sounds around the house. That strike of lightning must have been close. Another boom and the front door swings open. What the hell?

I move to go close it and make sure it's locked, but Beau is standing in the doorway.

"What are you doing here? I thought you weren't leaving for another," I glance at my phone. "Thirty minutes."

He takes a step in and closes the door behind him, locking it for good measure. "Why isn't the door locked?"

"I forgot?" I shrug my shoulders. "But seriously, what are you doing here?"

Him being in my space will make it that much harder for me to try to forget I kissed him.

He glances toward the living room. "I know how much you hate storms, and I wanted to make sure you weren't alone." He gestures toward the coffee table and laughs. "I see you're prepared, though."

"Shut up." I smack him on the shoulder. "I'd offer you food, but all I have is frozen pizza. I can make you one."

"I'm good." He grabs my hand and leads me toward the sofa. "Besides, there's something I need to tell you."

"Nothing good ever follows those words."

"This is good, I promise." He sits down and pulls me to sit next to him. "You know how I prepared those marketing plans for you?"

"Yeah." Lot of good they'll do since my brother turned down the idea. "Hopefully they didn't take too much of your time."

"That's the thing, Piper. My boss wants me to work on it with you to see if it can be done on a minimal budget. And I could get a promotion out of it."

"That's amazing." It is, and I'm so freaking happy he's

getting this opportunity. But that means I'll be spending even more time with him. Tamping down my feelings for him over the years has been easy, until I freaking kissed him. Now everything feels awkward. At least, it does on my end.

"So are you cool with moving forward with it."

"Absolutely." What else can I say? I'd be a shitty best friend if I said no. Especially when he's supported every idea I've ever had. Now I need to figure out how to cast these feelings I have for him aside. Once and for all. I'll ask whoever pops up on my dating app next on a date. It's the only way.

eight

. . .

beau

SHE SAYS she's excited to work on this marketing plan with me, but her face doesn't match the delivery. Most people wouldn't be able to tell, but I know her expressions. The one she has right now says she's agreeing under duress.

"You can say no." I squeeze her hand. "It won't hurt my feelings. But this is a way we can try the things you want with no budget and it'll help both of us out."

How we're going to do it without her brother knowing is another story entirely. But she also doesn't know that her brother gave me a warning about letting her go through with her ideas. I don't want her to lose her job. At the same time, this is the perfect way to prove to him her ideas are solid.

There's a boom in the distance and she scoots closer to me. Practically in my lap. As shocked as she was that I came, it's probably a good idea I'm here. She shouldn't be in the storm alone.

"I've got you," I whisper into her hair.

"Just like always," she replies. "And it's not that I don't want to do this whole marketing thing. I do, more than anything."

"But?" If I don't prompt her with questions, she'll beat around the bush without actually getting to the point of what she wants to say.

"But," she drawls. "Pierce is already mad about the stories I posted the other night. He hasn't come out and said anything directly to me, though. Parker showed up at my house to let me know."

"I can see how that would be a problem." There's no way that's the only reason. She lives to test her boundaries with her brother. "Is there anything else?"

The rain picks up momentum. The drops are loud against the roof and I already know I'm going to be here for a while.

Piper moves away from me and picks up the lighter on the coffee table. One by one she lights the candles on the table, preparing for a possible power outage. She has more to say. This small talk is only so she can put it off a tad longer and gather her thoughts.

"Piper?"

She sets down the lighter but doesn't face me. She's hunched over so far, I'm worried her hair might touch the flames. My hand moves of its own volition to tuck the strands away, but I stop. Any sudden movement may break whatever she's about to say.

"It's just that things are awkward now…since the other night." She doesn't have to say when she kissed me. We both know what she's referring to. "Spending that much time together could make things even more weird, and I don't want anything to jeopardize our friendship."

"So, you have been avoiding me?" The words are out of my mouth before I can stop them. At least I know I was right. Not that I doubted myself.

"Maybe?" She shrugs and leans back. "Ugh, I've ruined everything by kissing you."

"Hey, I'm still here, aren't I?" I wrap an arm around her shoulder. The same way I've done a million times before, and she sinks into the embrace. "You haven't ruined anything. We will always be best friends. Kiss or no kiss."

Another crack of thunder permeates the air. This time I can see sparks in the night sky. Seconds later the TV and every single light in the house goes dark. She must have a sixth sense with lighting the candles.

"Well, she leans her head on my chest. I'm definitely glad you're here right now."

"So, we'll work the marketing plan?" Yes, I'm like a dog with a bone, but I need to know how to move forward. Pierce will be a problem. Hopefully, I can handle that without causing too much fuss. Who knows, he might not have a problem with it if it isn't going to cost the winery any money.

"Yes." I can almost feel her rolling her eyes. "We'll do the marketing plan. It has to be under the radar as much as possible, though. Pierce will blow a gasket if he finds out I'm going behind his back again."

She's not wrong. He's not much for giving people space to do their jobs how they see fit. He always has to have his finger in the process.

"We'll figure it out." That's the one thing she doesn't

have to worry about. I'll do everything in my power to make sure she doesn't get the brunt of his disapproval.

"I guess this means you're staying the night?" She lifts her head back to see my reaction.

"Won't that be awkward?" Is it shitty of me to throw her words back in her face? Absolutely. Do I care when she's this close to me and in my arms? Not in the slightest.

"Shut up." She head butts me in the chest. "I mean you're already here. There's no power and I do not want to spend the evening alone in a dark house."

"Still scared of the dark? I thought you outgrew that ages ago."

She snorts and it's the cutest sound. Most people wouldn't agree. It's a good thing I'm not most people.

"I did until I moved out on my own. It's creepy out here with no lights or sound." She glances out the window and shivers despite the heat. "If I didn't know better, I'd think this whole piece of land is haunted."

The laugh bubbles out of my chest. "How many times have we talked about this. Nothing is haunted. It's just the trees making weird noises."

"Doesn't fix the creepy factor." Her phone buzzes beside me and she reaches around to grab it before glancing at the screen. "My brother is an idiot."

She shows me the text and I shake my head.

Parker: Hey scaredy cat. Need me to come down there and chase the ghosts away. Or at least bring a generator?

Piper: No. I'm good. Beau's here.

Parker: Of course he is. Hi Beau. I know you're reading this over her shoulder.

She locks the screen and tosses the phone to the other end of the couch.

"He knows us too well." I chuckle.

"Or he thinks he does." She argues. "So, what do you want to do? Whatever it is, it can only be done by candlelight, obviously."

There isn't really much we can do. "Do you still have the boardgames and cards in the closet?"

"Yeah. I don't know if everything is there, though. Peter got mad when he was losing one night and threw a bit of a tantrum."

I shift her to the side and leave the couch. "I'll go get them. If anything, we can pass the time with card games, even if all the pieces aren't there."

Piper shrugs and pulls the blanket from the back of the couch, wrapping it around her. "It's better than sitting in the dark bored."

As much as I'd love to make things interesting as we play whatever games I can find, I don't want to press my luck too much. She's on board with the marketing plan and hopefully doesn't feel embarrassed about the kiss anymore. Not that she should in the first place. Right now, everything feels like it did before that night, and I don't want to ruin it.

Ugh. I'm too old for this shit. Sleeping on the floor never bothered me as a kid, but now…it's not so great on the back. If we would have gone to Piper's room like I suggested, I wouldn't be in this situation. She refused to leave the living room because it was too dark in her room. It's a valid fear. Especially way out here in the country.

Actually, I probably would have still ended up on the

floor. She's pretty insistent on the we're only friends thing. Sleeping in the same bed would not have been a good idea. As much as I hate to admit it, she may be right. With us working on this marketing plan together, we'll be together a lot more.

Even though this project is work adjacent, I still need to treat her as if she was one of my clients. Letting her know how I feel about her…how I've felt about her for years, would be a conflict of interest. My only course of action right now is to shove all those feelings deep inside. I've managed to bury them for this long. How hard can it be?

First things first, I need to see if the electricity is back on. I cross my fingers as I get up and make my way to the light switch. Flicking it up, I wait for the light to come on…nothing. Piper won't be happy about this.

Shuffling sounds come from the couch and I turn to find Piper stretching. Her t-shirt rises a few inches exposing the skin beneath. Stop it, Beau. Friends only. Remember That.

"Power is still out."

"Ugh. I hope this isn't an all-day thing." She searches for her phone. "I'm sure if I'm out the rest of the family is out, too."

Her phone is sitting on the coffee table next to the deck of cards. We may have been in an intense game of go fish before we decided to go to sleep. I pick it up and hand it to her. "Here you go."

She taps on the screen to unlock it and groans. "Yep. Everyone on the land is out of power, including the winery. Apparently, there's damage outside and Pierce wants us to help with clean up."

"I hope it's not a lot of damage." I run my hand

through my hair. If it is, it could set the company back months.

"Pierce's text doesn't sound urgent." She shrugs and sets the phone down. "I'll head over there in an hour or so. It's too early to deal with all of them."

"Did he close the winery for the day?"

"Yeah. At least we got all those orders out yesterday. Hopefully they made it to their destinations okay."

"What orders? I thought y'all didn't do a ton of shipments and most of it was walk-ins."

"It was weird. When I came in yesterday the system had about ten online orders. I helped Pierce get them out the door since we were closing early."

"Oh. That's pretty cool." A small part of me wonders if it's because of the social media posts. In my gut, I know it's true. She'll wave it away as people wanting to wind down.

"Yep."

I bend down to grab my blanket since it seems the order conversation is over. Just as I'm about to fold the corners together, my phone rings. I have no idea who could be calling me. I check the name and tilt my head to the side. Why the hell is Cole calling me?

"Hello?"

"Hey, man. I don't know if you've checked your email yet, but Mr. Gardner said if you're affected by the storms that came through last night, you can have a paid day off to take care of things."

It's cute how he says Mr. Gardner to sound like he's equal to the rest of us.

"Oh, okay."

"Just thought I'd let you know before you came into work. Is it bad your way? We didn't get much here."

"I'm actually not sure. I haven't checked for damage yet."

"Hopefully you didn't. Just let Mr. Gardner know what you're doing."

"Thanks for the heads up."

I hang up the phone and immediately check my email. It's not that I don't believe Cole, but I want to make sure.

Sitting at the top is an email from my boss. I tap out a quick response and shove my phone in my pocket.

Piper glances up at me. "Is everything okay?"

"Yep. Looks like I'll be able to help y'all with the clean up today."

"No work?"

"Not if we were affected by the storms. And since the Summers family is practically my own, I think that's a good enough reason."

"You don't have to help." She watches my reaction. "It's not like you're an employee."

"I know, but the more hands you have, the faster it gets done." I finish folding the blanket. "I'm gonna go check on my house and see if I can find us some breakfast. Surely someone in town has power."

Her stomach picks that exact moment to growl, and she wraps her arms around herself in embarrassment. I don't know why since I've seen her inhale an entire pizza by herself.

"Food is probably a good idea." Her gaze moves toward the kitchen and she shakes her head. "Sorry I'm not better prepared for power outages."

My laugh comes out loud and she jumps. "Let's be real,

Piper. You rarely have a stocked fridge. You're used to eating out or bumming leftovers from your parents."

"It's not my fault I suck at cooking." I raise my eyebrows at her, and she winces. "Okay, I have no interest in cooking. Is that better?"

"It's the truth, so yeah." I take stock of anything else that needs to be cleaned up in her house. Thankfully the sun is up and I don't have to rely on her flashlight.

"I can clean up my bed mess." She knows me so well.

"Okay. I'll be back. If you head to the winery before then, let me know and I'll meet you up there."

"Sounds good."

Leaving is the last thing I want to do right now, but we need to eat and I want to make sure my house didn't sustain any damage. I can feel her eyes on me as I walk toward the door, and there's not a single part of me mad about it.

nine

· · ·

piper

"WHY DO you keep looking down the driveway?" Parker asks as we grab some contractor bags.

Honestly, we should rent a dumpster. While the damage isn't as bad as it could have been, there's more than I was anticipating.

"Huh?" I heard him, but I'm giving myself time to answer. I know he'll give me crap after our conversation a few nights ago.

"You keep staring at the driveway. Why? Are you expecting someone?"

He just had to throw that in. It takes everything in me not to suffocate him with the bag in my hand.

"Beau is coming to help us with the cleanup." Before he has a chance to open his mouth and say something sarcastic, I add, "and he's bringing food."

"From where?" He glances at all the downed tree limbs

and various debris covering the property. "I'll be shocked if anyone in town has power."

"I never said it was for you. He's bringing me breakfast because I had nothing in my fridge."

"Maybe I'll text him and ask him to bring me something, too. Besides, outside of you, I think I'm one of his favorite people."

Pfft. He would think of himself that way. It's kind of annoying that he does in fact like Parker, though. Not that I blame him, outside of Paula, he's my favorite sibling.

I see a car creeping up the driveway and laugh. "Looks like you might be too late. I think he's already here."

"Lucky you," he grumbles and waves his trash bag in the air to open it. I don't think he meant for me to hear it.

"Yes, lucky me." I grin at him. "You should find yourself a best friend as amazing as mine."

He rolls his eyes and moves further away from me. It's just food. He has plenty at his house. He tends to keep his fridge well stocked. I would know, I've borrowed a few things from him on the off chance I decide to cook.

"I have plenty of friends," he scoffs. "I'm just not co-dependent with them."

Am I that way with Beau? Surely, he would say something if he thought I was being too much. I open my mouth to argue this point with my brother, but I hear footsteps behind me.

"I have breakfast." Beau's voice is chipper, and I can't deny hearing it brings me comfort. Even though I'm surrounded by family most days, he feels like…home.

I turn to face him and my jaw drops at the massive box in his hand. It doesn't have any logos on it, though. "Look,

I know I like to eat, but this feels like a lot for just the two of us."

He laughs and shakes his head. "I couldn't show up without food for everyone. That would make me kind of an asshole. Besides, I'm sure everyone else is hungry."

Parker has moved and isn't in Beau's line of sight. He sticks his tongue out at me, and I want to cut it off. He's going to throw this in my face for years. Gah, why does Beau have to be such a kind-hearted soul? Even though I'd do the same if I wasn't still bitter with my siblings.

"Do I, at least, get first dibs?" I don't even know what's in the box, but I'll be damned if Parker gets any food before I do.

He nods and holds the box in my direction. "Take as many as you want, I think I bought enough."

The edge of the tab gets caught on the slot when I try to open it one-handed. Dropping the trash bag, I use both hands to pry it open. A stack of foil wrapped goodies are tightly packed inside.

"Did you buy out the whole taco shop? And where did you find one that had power?"

I dig around to find my favorites. Two potato and egg, and one chorizo and egg. I'm sure I'll get more of the latter, most of the folks in my family don't like it.

He shrugs and turns toward Parker once I have my food in hand. "I had to go outside of Asheville. That's why it took me so long to get here. I think everyone in town had the same idea."

"Is your power out, too?" I feel like a jerk for just now asking. It should have been the first thing out of my mouth rather than food. Being hangry is a thing, though. And I'm on the verge of it.

"Nope. I guess my house is on one of the essential grid lines. Perks of living in town, I guess."

"Then you won't mind me staying at your place during the next big storm. As much as I love it out here, I'm not a fan of power outages when we get strong winds." I wave a hand toward the tree limbs littering the property. "And as you can see, the gusts got pretty high."

"As if you even have to ask." He shakes his head and makes his way toward the house we use as our main building. "Is everyone else inside? I don't want the food to get cold before they get a chance to eat."

"No," Parker butts in. "They are in the back. I think Dad and Pierce have been cleaning up for a while so they'll welcome the break."

We follow my closest sibling around the house to the backyard. Pierce is closing up a trash bag and sets it next to a pile of them. His eyes widen as he takes in the group of us before narrowing on me and Parker.

"I thought y'all were cleaning up the front, and yet, I see no full bags."

"We were getting started when Beau pulled up." Parker slaps him on the back. "He rescued us without even realizing it."

"I brought breakfast tacos if anyone is hungry." He lifts the box as an offering. "I didn't have to go in today and figured y'all could use another set of hands."

"Thanks." Pierce eyes him wearily. "Everyone, come eat." His voice is loud in the silence surrounding us.

"Dang, I think they heard you in the next county over." Was it necessary to be a smart ass? No. Do I enjoy needling him? Absolutely. At least this is all in good fun.

I'm still annoyed with him about the marketing plan.

Even though I'm doing it in secret with Beau. But if I act differently, he may suspect something is going on. The last thing I want to do is have him hyper focus on me.

"I can always be louder." He laughs.

Since Dad has been talking about handing the winery over to us, I don't think I've seen him laugh. Not that he has ever been jovial, but the humor has been few and far between. It's nice to hear the sound from him, even if it's startling.

"I think we're good." I grin.

All of my siblings descend on us. Beau avoids getting tackled and sets the box on the table we have set up for tastings. We have an area in the house as well, but this set up is for those nice evenings when it isn't too hot or cold.

It's actually the set from my parents' house. There are so many memories surrounding this table and every single one of them include Beau. From making a mess with s'mores to all of us laughing into the night over some prank Parker pulled. I hope we never get rid of it.

I grab an open seat before there aren't any left and unwrap my taco. "Can someone hand me the salsa?" They are delicious without it, but I'm a salsa girl through and through. I put it on pretty much everything.

"Here you go." Philip hands me a small bowl and plastic spoon. He grabs his tacos and takes another one of the seats. "What made you decide to give us a hand today?" His question is directed at Beau.

My best friend shrugs and takes the seat next to me. Our legs touch and a shiver flows through my body. It takes everything in me to shove aside any, and all, attraction I feel toward him.

"My boss said we could take off if we had any damage.

Y'all are basically family, and I figured you may need the help."

"Thank God," Philip sighs. "Any chance I can talk you into getting on the roof to see if there was any damage?"

"Hell no." He catches my mom's eyes and immediately slaps his hand over his mouth. A few seconds later he mumbles, "Sorry, Mrs. Summers."

"Please." She waves the apology away. "It's not like I haven't heard worse from my own children. At least you try to remember your audience."

"It's not like we go around throwing F bombs, Mom." I roll my eyes and take another bite.

"Maybe not you, but your brothers are a different story."

The brothers in question have the decency to look ashamed. Serves them right. Looks like I'm Mom's favorite for the moment. Although truth be told me and Paula have always been because we're the only girls in a house full of boys. We gave her just as much hell, though.

"Do we have to talk about bad habits right now?" Peter groans. "I promise I won't cuss in front of you again."

"Yeah, right." Mom rolls her eyes as she digs through what's left of the tacos.

Shockingly it's not super hot out here. I guess the rain brought down the temperature. Too bad it didn't take the humidity with it.

"You could always make it interesting." I wait to see if anyone will bite.

"What do you mean?" Peter leans forward in his chair.

"A swear jar." I shrug and watch the horror on my brother's face. "Then when it's full we can put that toward our next family vacation, or Mom can use it for a spa day."

"Absolutely not." Peter and Philip yell at the same time.

"I would be fine with that." Mom grins. "A day at the spa sounds lovely."

"You realize you'd probably be going weekly, right?" Philip laughs. At least he has a sense of humor about it.

"Our older brother said he wouldn't cuss in front of mom just moments ago. Why would you fill it up?"

"I think we all know us better than that baby sister."

Ugh, I hate when he throws that term around. I mean, it's what I am, but the way he says it makes it feel so demeaning. Like I'm less than because I'm the youngest.

"Time to get back to work." Pierce claps his hands together. "You two," he points at me and Parker. "At least pretend like you're doing something."

He knows the both of us well enough to know we're going to goof off while we work.

"I'm pretty sure I should take offense to that." Parker crumbles the foil in his hand. "For your information we work just as hard as the rest of you. But...we work smarter."

If that statement would have come from me, Pierce would have something to say. Since it's coming from the youngest brother, he brushes it aside. Figures. One day this family will realize my worth. Maybe it'll be too late when they do, and I'll move on to greener pastures like Paula.

I gather everyone's trash and put it in the closest trash bag. Mine is still up front and I turn to head back around the house. If Pierce can't see me, he can't ride my ass about how fast I'm working.

After a few steps, I realize my friend isn't following me. "You coming, Beau?"

He waves my question away. "I'll be up there in a bit. I need to grab a trash bag and see where Pierce wants me."

Weird. He never willingly talks to my eldest brother. Add the fact he brought breakfast for everyone and things aren't making sense. What is he up to?

ten

. . .

beau

THE HURT on Piper's face as she walked back to the front of the house stings. I'm not trying to blow her off. There are some things I need to talk to Pierce about.

Thoughts about how we were going to pull off this marketing ploy tumbled through my mind as I drove to my house earlier. We can't. It's the sad truth of the matter.

Piper will be furious with me when she realizes what I'm doing, but I can deal with that, maybe. What I can't handle is seeing her be berated by her brother. A topic I'll cover with him at a later time. She may be one of his employees, but she's also his sister. He doesn't have to treat her like shit to get his point across.

Now to find the brother in question. He was with our entire group moments ago, and he seems to have vanished. He's like a freaking magician when he wants to be.

I pick up the roll of trash bags and pull out two of

them. Shoving the end of one of them into my pack pocket, I open the other and begin my search for the eldest Summers' sibling.

He's nowhere near the main house where they see customers. That only leaves a few more places he could be. I peek into the building where the wine is made. It's pitch black and no source of light can be seen. He's not in here.

There's another building with the shipping supplies and bottles. It looks dark in there as well. He has to be outside somewhere. I have no idea what the hell I'm going to say to him. Maybe I should have prepared for this better.

I round the corner of the building. "Holy shit."

There are large pieces of metal sheeting littering the ground. Pierce said the damage was minimal. This looks anything but that.

"Keep it down." Pierce hushes me. "I don't want the others to see how bad it is over here. They'll freak out."

"Are you also not telling your parents?" It isn't my place, but this looks bad.

He rolls his eyes because of course he does. The arrogance Pierce holds never ceases to amaze me.

"Of course they know. Until Dad officially retires, he's still in on all the business stuff." He points toward the metal pieces he's stacked in a pile. "This is definitely business."

"I'll say." Hopefully the repairs don't take long or cost a ton of money. Not that they don't have it. I may have fibbed a bit to my boss. They have the dollars. Pierce doesn't want to put any of it into marketing.

"Why are you back here anyway? Shouldn't you be

helping my sister, or covering for her while you do all the work?"

See, these types of digs are unnecessary. Why does he always have to find something about her to put down? Unless, of course, he knows she could run circles around him.

The urge to fight back is overwhelming, and it takes everything in me to tamp down my anger. Getting into it with Pierce isn't going to make him agree to what I'm about to suggest.

Well, what I'll eventually propose. Right now, I need to get him in a better mood. I've learned how to work him… for the most part.

"I was going to say y'all are free to use my house for whatever you need. Showers, cooking, a nap." He doesn't miss the slight jab.

"Are you sure? I know Mom will probably want to get a hot shower as soon as possible."

"Of course. Your family has fed, clothed and dealt with me since I was thirteen. It's the least I can do."

He looks relieved. "Thanks. That means a lot. I'll let my parents know as soon as I head back to their house."

"No problem." I dig my heel into the soft ground and stare at the plush green grass beneath my feet. "There's one more thing."

Pierce grumbles for a few seconds. "If this is about Piper's plan, I already told both of you how I feel about it, and there's no changing my mind. She really needs to stop sending you to do her dirty work. It may have worked when you were teenagers, but you're grown now."

He's one to talk. "She doesn't know the reason I'm here."

"You aren't going to go back up front until I've heard what you have to say, are you?" He knows me well enough to figure this out.

"No." I shake my head. I have zero problems arguing with a brick wall if it means proving my point. Unless it's to Piper. I'll roll over for anything that woman says. Always have and will.

Resigned, he sighs. "Fine. Give me your spiel."

I tell him about what my boss wants and how this could be big for Starlit Fields. The partnership doors this could open up outside of the ones he's already formed.

"Basically, he wants me to test this plan with a low or no spend budget. But…it means you'll need to give Piper more creative freedom on social media."

He crosses his arms and stares me down. It's supposed to be intimidating, but he's never scared me. Honestly, I don't understand why his siblings let him push them around. But I don't have any, so maybe it's a different dynamic. Either way, I'm not letting him bully me.

"Why should I okay this? Especially after I told Piper no." His voice is stern, but not in the same way I've heard him speak to anyone else. Maybe it's because I'm not officially a family member, I just played one in school.

"Because in my professional opinion, I think it would do wonders for the winery. You'd be able to grow your business and curate the types of customers you want. Piper is completely capable of doing that. Considering how popular she was with only doing a short Q&A, I think she can do so much more."

"I don't know." Pierce lifts an arm and scratches the back of his neck. "Now isn't really a good time." He points to the metal pieces from the roof on the ground. "I won't even know if we can ship things. I haven't been inside to scope out the damage, and probably won't be able to until we get power."

"What do you have to lose, Pierce?" I throw my arms up. The fact he's coming around to the idea because I'm voicing them also pisses me off. When Piper told me about him and Paula coming to an agreement, I thought maybe he had changed…at least a little. I was clearly wrong.

He looks around the winery, taking it all in. The property is beautiful and if he'd open it up for more events, he'd be able to fill this place up. Cash flow wouldn't be an issue because people would book months, or years, in advance to have private parties here. They could get involved with the community. The possibilities are endless. But he's going to sit here and worry about nonexistent problems.

He sighs before meeting my eyes. "Fine. I'll let y'all do this on two conditions."

"What are they?" Please don't be anything that puts me in a compromising position.

"You have to run anything you do by me before you do it."

"Done."

"And Piper can't know that I know you're doing this."

Ugh, I was afraid this would be one of the stipulations. "Why?"

I know the answer, but I want to hear it from him. Then I'll know for sure it's because I came to him with the idea.

"Do you have any idea how much crap she'll give me if she knows I told you yes and her no? I don't have the mental energy to deal with it."

There it is. The answer that shows how much an ass he can be.

"Maybe you should think about why that is."

Without another word, I turn and head toward Piper. I'll keep the agreement a secret…for now. But I also know the predicament I've put myself in. I'll be lying to my best friend.

"You're house or mine?" I help Piper onto the passenger seat of my car. Both of us are covered in sweat. It felt nice when I first got to the winery, but as the day warmed up, the humidity hit us like a sucker punch.

"Well, considering there's still no power here, your house. I need a shower." She buckles her seatbelt and waits for me to get in the driver seat. "Actually, can we stop by my house first? I need to get clothes."

"Sure thing." I turn on the car and head down the driveway. That's the one perk of the Summers owning this large piece of property, everyone has a house on it with enough space they don't get on each other's nerves. Even Paula has a piece of the property. She doesn't use it, though.

It's not long before we are pulling into her driveway. Piper always goes on about how it's the greatest perk of living on the land her family owns. She doesn't even have to drive if she doesn't feel like it. But that rarely happens as far as I know. The weather would have to be perfect for her walk the fifteen to twenty minutes to the office. Which is a rare occurrence in Texas. Especially when we sometimes feel all the seasons in one day.

The limbs that covered the yard this morning are in a pile. She must have taken care of it before she left for the winery. Not that I blame her. I wouldn't want to clean up even more after doing it all day for work.

Little does she know, I was planning on helping her. I doubt her brothers had any intention of doing it. At least they didn't mention anything about it today while I was there.

"Do you want me to come in with you?"

"Nope," she shakes her head as she throws open the passenger door. "Give me five minutes."

I put the car in park and get out. I didn't check all the way around this house this morning. She probably did, but it doesn't hurt to take a second look.

None of the shingles came off her roof, but part of her fence is bent in the corner. When she first put it up, I asked her why she bothered. She said she might want to get a dog some day and it would need a place to roam. Five years later, and there's still no pets. This weekend I'll repair it with her.

She's walking out of the house as I make my way back to the car. "What were you doing?"

"Seeing if there was any other damage from the storm. The fencing is bent in the back."

"I know." She lifts her bag higher on her shoulder. "I forgot to tell you about it earlier. Didn't want Pierce to think I wasn't working hard."

"Your brother can get over himself." She slides into the passenger seat and closes the door. "And I'll help you repair the fence this weekend. It shouldn't be too hard."

"Thanks. You're keeping me from having to ask one of

my brothers for help. I don't know what I would do without you."

"Deal with their bullshit." I laugh. "You ready?"

"Yep." She reaches for the radio and turns it to a pop station before turning up the volume.

This small thing would probably annoy most people, but she's done it since we were in high school. Despite not really liking the music, I always give her power over the radio. She's forced to listen to stuff she doesn't care for at work, and I want her to be completely comfortable with me. Even if the dance music isn't my taste.

The ride to my house is mostly silent. We're about a mile away when I notice the music isn't as loud as it was seconds ago.

"Why were you looking for Pierce earlier?"

I knew she was going to ask, but I didn't think it would take her this long.

"I was letting him know everyone was free to shower or nap over here." I purposefully omit the other thing I talked to him about. And this reason isn't exactly a lie. I did tell him that.

"Oh." She sounds surprised.

"Why?"

"I thought you were going to tear him a new one for treating me the way he does."

Interesting. She doesn't want me to be her boyfriend, but she wants me to stand up for her like a boyfriend would. I mean, I did anyway. Best friends also fill that role of defense. Still...she seems upset I didn't defend her honor.

"If it means that much to you, I can still do that." I lift

my phone from the console and act like I'm opening my contacts list.

"No!" Her voice is loud in the small space. "Especially not when you're driving."

Pulling into my driveway, I put the car in park. "Are you sure? I'm not driving anymore."

"Oh my God, yes, I'm sure. He probably hears it enough from me."

"Probably." I shrug and open the door. "But another voice is never a bad thing."

"It is if it's against my moody brother. You know how much he holds grudges. It took him forever to try to mend things with my sister."

"You're not wrong." I get out of the car and hurry over to her side. As soon as Piper is out of the car, I grab her bag and lift it onto my shoulder. "What the hell do you have in here? Are you moving in, and I didn't get the memo?"

She scoffs and rolls her eyes. "I didn't ask you to get my bag. But no, it has everything I need in case I'm here longer than one night."

The thought of her being here more than one night thrills me. We're at each other's houses all the time anyway, and she's stayed over a few times. But the fact that I can provide her a place to stay does big things for my ego.

As soon as I open the door to the house, I set her bag in the foyer. "You can take a shower first."

"Absolutely not." She's shaking her head. "I know how you get when I use all the hot water."

This is proof of how comfortable she is with me. Why

can't she see we'd be great together. Or maybe she knows but she's too scared to take that leap.

"Fine, I'll take a quick shower. Then you can hop in."

"I'll search your kitchen for food. Or see if anyone in town has power yet. I'm guessing they do."

"Sounds good." I don't tell her how badly I hope she finds a restaurant with power. I love her more than anything, but Piper is not skilled in the kitchen.

We just need to get through the night without making things between us awkward. I can do that. At least I hope I can.

eleven

. . .

piper

BEAU DID everything in his power last night to go over the marketing plans. It's not that I didn't want to, but I was exhausted after cleaning up at Starlit Fields.

Pierce left a message on my phone this morning. The winery is closed another day, but we don't need to come in. He has contractors looking at the roof of one of the warehouses. I didn't even know there was damage.

Beau is in the living room when I walk in. "Good morning." My hands are lifted putting my hair into a ponytail.

"Good mo—" The greeting cuts off and his mouth drops open as soon as he sees me.

I glance down to see what has him so flustered and realize I'm wearing what I normally do when I'm alone at home. A long t-shirt with nothing underneath. Not even registering that it's also slightly shorter because my arms are up.

I immediately put my hands down, letting my hair fall around my face. What I'm wearing didn't even register when I got up. I should have at least thrown on some leggings.

"I'll, uh, be right back." I rush back to the guest room and slam the door behind me. Spending even more time with him while marketing the winery is going to be torture. The way his eyes trailed along my body while he sat there with his mouth wide open is something I don't know that I'll ever get out of my head.

I should have stayed with one of my brothers. Or, hell, even Paula. Then I wouldn't be mortified to walk back out there and act like he wasn't looking at me like I was a dessert.

This will not end well for either of us. I can already tell. The more he looks at me like I'm his, the less I'll be able to resist taking things a step further.

"Piper? Are you okay in there?" There's a soft knock on the door.

Shit. I lean my head against the door as silently as possible. I don't want him to know how small the distance is between us. If I don't answer him, he'll barge in. It's the one thing I can count on from him. Beau is the only person who has been able to read me this well.

I quietly slide away from the door and move closer to the disaster on top of the bed. My clothes are scattered everywhere. There's another knock. My best friend is getting impatient, but I had to put some physical space between us.

"I'm fine, Beau." My voice is panicked even though I try my hardest to keep it level and disinterested.

Approximately two minutes. That's how long I have

until he'll walk through the door. I should have locked it when I came in. This is why I live alone. I could never remember to lock anything after myself. Hell, I don't even lock my front door half the time.

My clothes fly off the bed as I shuffle through them trying to find a pair of leggings. Shorts. Anything to put under this shirt and stop Beau from looking like he wants to eat me up. Not that I'd mind. Stop thinking like that Piper. You are friends. Only. Friends.

My fingers grip around an item that feels like my workout clothes, and I pull it out just as I hear the doorknob turn. They make a popping noise as I shake them out and slide my legs through. I'm pulling them up just as the door opens.

Thank God, I got them up before he came all the way in. But I'm not completely steady and I teeter backward while adjusting my waistband.

Before I know it, an arm is wrapped around my back and pulling me forward. Ugh. This is going to be one of those days full of embarrassment, I can already feel it. Since I've known him, I've never responded to him in this way. Well, maybe those first couple of days on the bus when we were getting to know each other, but definitely not since then. The only difference between then and now…the freaking kiss.

"I thought you said you were good." He laughs before letting me go. His fingers sliding across the sliver of skin above my waist. My body shivers in delight. Resisting him is going to be harder than I thought. Even though I know that touch was completely innocent.

"I am." I huff and pull my shirt down. "You opened the door and scared me."

"You know well enough if you don't answer I'm coming in."

"Yeah, yeah," I wave him away. "You should have grown out of that by now. Besides, my brothers aren't in the room torturing me."

"I mean, they could have been. They would never let you answer when we were kids. The only way I could come to your rescue was if I came in unannounced." He shrugs and walks out of the room. "What's on the agenda for today?"

"Nothing. I need to clean out my fridge and see when the power comes back. My brother said we're closed again. Something about there being damage on the shops and contractors coming out to look at it."

"Hopefully, they can get the repairs done quickly." I can barely hear him as he's making his way to the living room.

"What did you say?" My steps are quick as I follow after him.

Guilt washes over his face. "I hope the repairs are done quickly."

"You knew there was damage to some of the buildings?"

Beau all of a sudden finds the floor more interesting than anything I'm wearing. "I saw it yesterday when I was looking for him. He asked me not to say anything because he didn't want you worrying."

"Of course he did." I brush past Beau, knocking into his shoulder. "You shouldn't have kept that a secret. We don't do that." Some other expression flashes across his face, but I can't tell what it is. "My brother should have told the rest of us, too. He seems to forget that we will all own the winery equally. Omitting problems is not good for the business, and makes me think he'll never see the rest of us as partners."

"He probably didn't want y'all to feel any added stress." He shrugs as if it's not a big deal.

It is, though. We'll never make it as a business unless he starts treating the rest of us like we are valuable to the winery. At least Dad humors us when making decisions.

"I guess." It's the only thing I can say. Mostly I don't want to fight with Beau, and this would definitely lead to one. "Since we're closed again today, any chance you can run me home on your way to work?"

"As if you have to ask." He grins over at me. "Let me know when you're ready. I've already let my boss know I'd probably be late."

"How did you know?"

He raises an eyebrow. "Seriously? I keep telling you I know you better than you know yourself sometimes."

It's not completely untrue. Except when it comes to wanting to take things a step further than friendship. There's no way I can take that leap. Everything between us will change.

"What are you doing here?" Parker's voice rumbles through the building, and I jump, dropping my phone in the process. Fucking Parker. I bend down to pick it up and inspect it to make sure there's no damage.

"Why does it matter? Last time I checked I work here."

On the way to my house this morning, Beau and I talked about the images and videos I need to get. It's one of the few things I can get done without him. Since nobody is supposed to be here today, I figured this would be the perfect opportunity.

"Yeah, but we're closed today. Or, did you not get Pierce's message?" He's eyeing the phone in my hand knowing damn well what the answer to that question is.

"I got the message." Why can't he leave me be? I'm not doing anything illegal. "Why are you here?"

"Because I saw your car in front of the office when I was heading to town." He leans against one of the barrels. "Now, it's your turn."

My brother isn't going to let up. It's one of the annoying things about the two of us. We're persistent when it comes to getting to the bottom of things.

"I need to get some video for the social media channels. There's just enough sunlight coming through that I don't have to worry about the lack of power."

"Does Pierce know you're doing this? I thought he nixed your marketing plan."

"He did." I turn to get a better angle of the shot I'm trying to film. "I'm doing it anyway. If he doesn't have to tell us about things going on with the winery, I don't have to divulge what I'm doing with our social accounts. And you better not tell him anything."

Now Parker moves toward me instead of hiding in the corner. "What are you talking about?"

"Did you know about the building damage prior to Pierce's text this morning? Or, am I the only one who never gets told anything?"

I swear if I'm the only one left out of the loop, I'm going to lose my shit.

Parker takes a couple of steps back. There must be

something in my demeanor that warns him away. He's probably scared I'll take a swing. As much as I'd like to say he's wrong, I can't. He's one of the few siblings who can correctly guess my mood.

"I knew, but only because I saw it last night when I was walking the grounds to make sure we got all the debris picked up. When I told Dad, he said Pierce already had it handled."

"Don't you think that's bullshit?"

"What?"

I throw my hands in the air. Why must he be so freaking obtuse?

"The fact that our big brother doesn't think he needs to give us important information about the winery. He acts like we're children instead of keeping us informed. It's not like we would have gotten mad or anything. But knowing what was going on is better than not."

"I kind of get it." Parker holds his hands up in surrender at my scowl. "Let me explain before you beat my ass. Dad has been raising Pierce to be the one in charge since we were kids. Does it suck? Yes. But in the end, we all should have equal say and knowledge. Maybe it's something we can bring up at the next weekly meeting."

"That's actually a good idea." For once he has a solution to a problem. Maybe I should talk to the rest of the siblings before then to see how they feel. If we come to him as a unified front, it's possible things will change.

"So, what does all this filming lead to?" He points to the phone in my hand. "I've never really thought about what people on social media do."

Of course he hasn't. He gets online and watches videos then sends me the ones he thinks are funny. That's the extent of his social media usage. I guess it's a good thing he's not in charge of all this. It's probably a good thing Pierce isn't either. He's gotten on his socials maybe once and never looked at it again.

"Well, I'll take these videos and either do a voice over or put text over them. It's just something to give people the vibe of our winery. If they like it enough, they'll either place an online order, or come visit us in person."

"That sounds like a lot of work." He scratches his head.

"It can be. But I love doing it. So, for me, it's not really work."

"Oh." He glances around the space no doubt wondering how I'm going to be creative with anything in here. "I'm gonna go." He points his thumb toward the door.

"Actually, I could use your hands for a bit."

"Excuse me, what?"

"Since you know about this secret, I need your hands to do a video."

"What exactly do I have to do? It's not going to be weird, is it?" Concern flashes across his face.

"No," I shake my head. "It's not going to be weird. I need you to pour the wine into a glass. Either straight from the tap or from a bottle. It doesn't matter."

"Won't Pierce notice if a bottle is gone from inventory?"

Ugh, he's making this harder than it should be.

"He would if we were using a bottle from here, but I planned ahead and brought my own." I reach down to the shelf in front of me and grab the bottle. "If you're lucky I'll even let you drink the wine."

"What do you need me to do?" He glances around the room to find a spot to set a glass he doesn't yet have.

I grab a glass from the shelf. It's not too big and has our logo on it. All the more reason to use it. Plus side, Pierce will never know it's missing because we have a ton of them. We give them to customers when they come in for tastings, or when they buy a certain number of bottles. At least he knows how to play up the customer service in that regard.

"We actually need to go outside for this." With the wine and glass in hand, I lead my brother out of the building and to the old wooden spool we have set up outside. Setting the glass and bottle down, I pull the wine opener out of my pocket.

"Where do I stand?" He asks as he eyes the bottle. I guess booze is always a good motivator.

I take a minute to walk around the spool, checking for where the shadows will hit. I don't want it to be too dark. Fun and flirty is the vibe I'm going for. Thank goodness, Parker fits that criteria. My other brothers would be too serious and ruin everything.

"Stand right here." I point to the left side. "And don't worry, I won't show your face. It'll be chest down."

"O-okay." His voice has a tremor in it. Who knew the charismatic person would be nervous about a video.

I pick up my phone, flip to the camera app and start recording. "Go ahead and open the wine. Then pour it like we would for a tasting."

"I can do that." He picks up the corkscrew. "Shit. Will they hear all this talking?"

"No. I'll edit it out. Now pour."

He does as I ask and I zoom in on the glass as he's pouring. This is going to be perfect for our socials. Hopefully, Beau thinks so, too. This zero-budget marketing is going to be interesting, but I'm up for the challenge.

twelve

. . .

beau

WORK IS the last place I want to be. The only good thing is Mr. Gardner was pleased with the progress Piper and I have made. It's not a lot, but I saw some of the videos she's posted. They turned out better than I expected. She's always had a creative eye for things, and her posts show it.

I wonder how she managed to get them without her brother seeing her. As far as she knows we're doing this in secret, even though it pains me keeping it from her. I know nothing good will happen when she finds out. Pierce better be around to back me up when it does. Piper holds grudges like nobody I've ever known. She's still mad at a girl we went to school with for telling everyone her birthday party theme was dumb.

Thirty minutes, that's all I have to last before I can go home and hang out with Piper. Until then, I better look at the analytics from the new posts. They don't have all the data I need, but it'll give me an idea if what she's doing is working. This is probably my favorite part of the job, especially if things are going in the direction I want.

"Hey." Cole slams his hand on my shoulder. I swear if this guy keeps doing shit like this, I'm going to punch him. "What are you working on?"

"The marketing numbers for that project I'm doing." He doesn't really need to know anything. This whole thing is between me and Mr. Gardner. The only reason I'm for sure going through with it is because Cole opened his big mouth. "Is there something you need?"

"Oh, yeah." He leans against the cubicle wall and crosses his arms. "We're going out for drinks after work and wanted to invite you."

This is new. Most of the guys here go out for drinks at least once a week, but they've never invited me or any of the women who work here. Honestly, their lack of invitation to all the employees says a lot about them and I really don't want to go. The only reason they're asking now is because Mr. Gardner wants me to see this marketing campaign through. If I have the ear of our boss, then it puts them closer to moving up the ladder. Too bad for them, I don't like being used as a pawn.

"Sorry, I can't. I have plans tonight." It's not a lie, but I can see the disappointment written all over Cole's face. His problem, not mine.

"Maybe some other time."

"Sure." What the hell else am I supposed to say? He put me on the spot and it's not like I can come out and say no. Office politics and hierarchy annoys me, but even I know I need to at least play nicely.

"Sounds good, man." He moves away from my desk.

"I'll see when we're going out again so you can check your calendar."

Little does he know, I plan on being busy every time he asks. Which reminds me, I need to find out what time Piper is supposed to come by. I grab my phone from my desk and shoot off a quick text.

BEAU

What time will you be at my house?

I put my phone down and continue analyzing the numbers she sent me. She usually takes a while to respond because she's too busy running around making sure nobody else needs her to do something. They really don't realize how much she does for them in all aspects of the business.

My phone vibrates faster than I expected.

PIPER

Sorry, I can't make it tonight.

BEAU

Did something happen at the winery?

PIPER

No. I forgot I have a date.

You have to be kidding me. She wants her brothers to take what she's doing seriously, but goes out on dates instead of showing up. I can't tell her that, though. Maybe my opinion is also a bit biased. The only person I want her date is me, and she does everything in her power to make sure we're strictly in the friend category. Frustration doesn't begin to explain everything I'm feeling right now.

> No problem. Let me know if anything changes.

The one thing she knows she can always count on is that I'll be there no matter what. Maybe I should make myself less available to her. Even the thought sends a pang through me. Why in the hell did I have to fall for my best friend all those years ago?

"What can I get you?" Eric leans across the bar with a shit eating grin on his face. The one I know means he's about to meddle.

There's no way I'm letting him interfere in my life. He has a habit of thinking he's everyone's matchmaker. I don't need it. I know who my match is. She needs to wake up and realize it for herself.

"The usual."

"Food and drink?"

"Sure."

Normally, they'd move me to a table if I'm ordering food, but it's a weeknight and slow. There's no reason for me to go to another spot. He walks to the small window and tells them my order. Patrick, the guy in charge of the kitchen, sees my face and gives me a sympathetic nod.

What is it with the people working here thinking I need comfort? I'm usually much better at hiding my emotions. After all, I've had a ton of practice over the years pretending I'm not in love with Piper. I didn't even realize she was still going on the dating apps after the last disaster. One day she'll wake up and realize I'm right in front of her.

Eric slides my beer in front of me. "Here you go. You want to talk about it?"

"Nope." It's a bit snarky, but it'll get him off my back for a bit.

"I'll bring over your food in just a bit."

A curt nod is all I can give him. I don't much feel like talking to anyone. Right now, Piper is on a date with some douchebag and I'm here drowning my sorrows because it's not with me. The guy she's with is probably nice… maybe. That's beside the point.

She won't even consider she has feelings for me. The kiss we shared a few weeks ago is proof she does. For once I wish she'd listen to her heart over her head. Things wouldn't change between us. We'd still be best friends. We'd just have added benefits.

"Where's the other half?"

I groan at the sound of Parker's voice. Of course, he's the person who would run into me while I'm pining for his sister. At least it's not one of the other brothers. We're cool and all, but I don't know how they'd react to my feelings for Piper.

"She's on a date," I mumble.

"I'm guessing that's why you're here giving everyone don't come near me vibes." He takes a seat on the stool next to me.

"Doesn't look like it's working." I take another sip of my beer before glancing over at him.

"I'm sure it works on everyone else, but I don't care." He waves toward Eric who is already working on his drink. Perks of being a regular, I guess. "Besides, everyone loves me."

"You're kind of full of yourself."

"Nah." He waves my comment away. "I just go after what I want."

"Doesn't mean you're not cocky about it."

"Touché." He nods as Eric slides over his whiskey. "So, how's your little project with my sister going?"

Fuck. How did he find out? Pierce left me with the impression nobody else would know what we were doing.

"I don't know what you're talking about."

"Calm down. She told me when I caught her taking a video. I'm guessing she didn't tell you."

"No." I guess it slipped her mind. It makes me feel slightly better about keeping my own secret, but only just.

"Why do you look like someone just kicked your puppy?" He bumps his shoulder into me.

"What are you talking about? I'm perfectly fine." Eric brings me another beer and the wings he knows I always get. "See." I point to my food. "I have my drink and food. There's nothing wrong."

"Soooo, my sister being on a date with someone who I'm sure is probably an asshole has nothing to do with the scowl you're wearing. Good to know."

"Fine." I throw my hands in the air knowing damn well I won't be able to eat in peace until he gets to the bottom of my mood. He's always been like this so I shouldn't be surprised. "Yes, I'm annoyed your sister is on yet another date that's going to turn into a disaster. I don't think she's gone on more than one with anyone she meets on these apps. She kissed me a couple of weeks ago and refuses to admit she feels anything for me. So, yeah, her being out with someone other than me is a problem."

"Damn, he got that out of you with a quickness." Eric laughs as he leans against the bar. "Maybe he should take my title as matchmaker and problem solver."

"Shut up, Eric. I don't need your shit, too." I take a long swig of my drink to avoid their gaze.

"Wait, back up." Parker turns toward me. "My sister kissed you?"

Why does his surprise sound fake?

"Yes." There's not one ounce of guilt in my response even though I know I should tread lightly with her brothers.

"I know, but damn, she's giving you the cold shoulder now. That's gotta suck." He laughs and that annoys me more. He sucks at acting. Maybe I should tell him that.

"Not really, but she's not willing to move past friend territory. She's worried it will make things weird."

Eric leans in even further. "I'm surprised it took her that long to kiss you. I've seen the two of you interact, and it's not like normal friends."

"In her defense, she was excited and a little tipsy."

Eric shakes his head and moves down the bar to serve another patron. Parker lets me eat in peace. I don't see where they are coming from. We've never acted like anything but friends. It's no different than the way Paula is around her coworkers at the flower shop.

We are comfortable with each other. As we should be since we've been friends since seventh grade. Never mind the fact I've had to bite my tongue every time she's gone on and on about how crappy her various boyfriends were. I'm no saint, I dated when we were in high school, but even then, I didn't fill her in on any details. It made me feel like crap so I didn't want to do it to her in case she had even a sprout of feelings for me.

"You look like you're thinking awfully hard over there," Parker says. Honestly, I thought he gave up on conversation with me and left.

"Not really. Just replaying some moments in my mind."

"I swear to God if you say anything about you and my sister kissing, I'm gonna puke."

Now that brings out a chuckle. "As much as I don't want to see that. It'd be funny as hell. But no, just thinking about what Eric said."

"Please." He waves his hand in the air. "The two of you have been in love with each other since we were in high school. Y'all are just too stubborn to do anything about it."

He's wrong. I would have known if she felt anything toward me way back then. "If you say so."

"Oh my God." Parker throws his hands in the air and slams them back on the table. "You need to get your head out of your ass and go after what you want. We all know it's Piper. Now, what are you going to do about it?"

That's the question. She did remember to send me her location so I can see when she gets home. No, I shake my head, I can't crash her date. It'd be hilarious, though.

"Wow, I didn't think it would make you concentrate so hard."

"Shut up, Parker." There's no way he doesn't get off on making people uncomfortable. He's a good sport, at least. I feel like the same comment from Pierce or Peter would include a scowl.

I pull my phone out of my pocket and glance at the

lock screen picture. It's one we took a couple of months ago at a waterpark. I unlock the phone and tap on the messages.

Beau

I don't know if you have any plans this weekend, but do you want to hit up the fair and carnival?

It's something the town does every year to get the kids excited about the upcoming school year. We used to go to it all the time in high school just to hang out and have some fun. Neither of us cared about the school related activities. Maybe I can recreate some of that and have it work in my favor.

This weekend...I'm going to tell her how I feel.

thirteen

. . .

piper

THE MESSAGE from Beau is like a ghost that haunts me. Normally, I'd text him back right away, but the invitation to the carnival this weekend came out of nowhere.

It doesn't help that he texted me while I was in the middle of a date. That's the problem, though. The date wasn't horrible and he wants to see me again. We had a great time bowling of all things. He didn't get mad when I beat him in the first game, which was a win for him. We had a great time. But…he's not Beau.

Being at the bowling alley reminded me of all the times Beau and I would drive to the next town over to play. That was our idea of Friday night fun. We went to the occasional party and hung out with people from school, but we felt most ourselves when it was just us. We didn't have to force conversation, or try to explain one of our inside jokes.

All of that is why I'm having a hard time saying yes to

another date, and haven't answered my best friend. It's not like I have anything better to do, and if anything, I can also hand out business cards. Why does everything have to be so confusing?

The whole reason I went on the date was to get my mind off Beau and try to push down my feelings toward him. Instead, all I kept thinking about was that text. It's all I've been able to think about today, too.

"So, what's going on with you and Beau?" Parker is an entire jump scare. I swear I'm going to put a damn bell on him. Or, I need to not be lost in my thoughts. That's probably the biggest factor. Even when I have music playing, he's never scared me as much as he has the past few weeks.

"He's my bestie?" Forming that as a question won't make things any easier when dealing with my brother. "And we're working on the marketing thing together."

He raises an eyebrow, knowing damn well I'm holding out. Has he noticed the change in dynamics between us? Things are normal, but there has been an energy when we're around each other that wasn't there before. It's like me kissing him opened up a floodgate, and it's been impossible to close it.

Thankfully, he seems like he's letting it go since there isn't a quick rebuttal. "How was your date last night?"

Or maybe not. "How did you know I had a date last night?"

The only person I told was Beau. As much as I love my siblings, I don't need them meddling in my dating life. It's part of the reason it's been years since I've brought anyone home for them to meet. Unless there's a high chance of exclusive dating, there's no reason to introduce them to my family.

"How do you know I was on a date? I could have been hanging out with friends."

"What friends?" He laughs and sits in the chair across from me. "Outside of Beau, the only people you willingly hang out with are family members."

"Then how do you know that?" Unless he's secretly following me.

"I ran into Beau last night. It's not often I see him at Out of the Ashes alone."

That is odd. He's not really a large crowd type of person. Why in the world would he go there by himself? I make a mental note to get to the bottom on it.

"We don't spend every second of the day together."

"Damn near," he replies.

He makes us sound co-dependent. I mean I guess in some ways we might be, but also not really. We're capable of doing things and making decisions without the other. Being each other's person when things are great, and falling apart, is a part of friendship.

"I don't know why you're so hung up on me and him being more than what we are. If we become anything else, it will ruin everything."

"Oh my God." He throws his hands in the air. "The two of you are exhausting and, both of you are in love with each other but refuse to do anything about it."

"Of course, I love him." I wave away his comment. "He's been a part of my life for over ten years. How could I not?"

He shakes his head as if he knows he's fighting a losing

battle. I'm not sure how he wants me to react, or what he wants me to say.

"Are you going to the carnival thing with him this weekend?" Before I even have a chance to open my mouth, he mimics a keep it shut motion with his hand. "The two of you need to figure your shit out before it implodes."

"It sounds like you're speaking from experience." I lean back in my chair and set my feet on the desk. The need to do something to hide what I feel. Because he's right. Beau and I are at a tipping point whether or not I want to admit it.

"Oh, hell no." He shakes his head as he walks toward the door. "Relationships aren't for me. Learned that lesson back in high school. I'm perfectly fine with hookups."

"One day you're going to meet someone who will change your mind."

"I hope not." He laughs and steps into the hallway before turning back. "Look, I love both you and Beau. At this point he's practically family. You need to stop being afraid and tell him how you feel. Both of you are getting on my nerves about this."

"I feel like he's my best friend." I roll my eyes and look anywhere but at my brother.

"Liar." Without accusation, he's out of my sight. He disappears as quickly as he appears.

He's not completely wrong, and it sucks that he knows it. Why can't he be the big sibling who tells me what I want to hear? I have other siblings who will give it to me straight. Except that's not what I need from him.

Going to the fair before school started was something we used to do when we were in school. Maybe it's time to bring some of that joy back into my life. We can get on the rides and pretend we don't have a care in the world, just like when we were kids.

I search around my desk for my phone and open up our text thread.

PIPER

Yes. I'll go to the fair with you.

We can see how this goes, and if I pick up on him having more than platonic feelings for me, I'll make my move.

"Dad! Do you know where the business cards are?"

I walked up to his house to see if he knew where they were stashed because I can't find them anywhere. Now, I'm a hot and sweaty mess. I should have driven up here to avoid feeling like crap. The thinking time was worth it, though. Sometimes you just need a good walk to think things through. Especially when emotions are on the line. If I read any part of tonight wrong, it could be disastrous for my friendship.

Having fun with Beau at the carnival this weekend is the top priority, but if I can also do some hand-to-hand marketing that will be even better. Plus, it'll distract me from reading into things more than I should.

Dad rounds the corner from the kitchen as I'm making my way through the foyer. "They should be in the office where I normally keep them. Why?"

I don't miss the suspicion in his eye. He was in that meeting a few weeks ago and knows I'm not supposed to be doing extra marketing.

"I'm going to the back-to-school event this weekend and figured I could hand out business cards. Don't worry, I'm going to check with the mayor to make sure I can."

Not a lie, it's on my list of things to do after I find the cards. I don't want to ask for permission then not be able to deliver.

"Most of the people in Asheville know about us."

"Yeah, but what if there are people who moved here recently. They may not know about our amazing wine. Besides, this isn't going to cost the company anything but my time."

"Does Pierce know?"

Ugh, I hate how he's already reverting all decision making to the eldest child. He isn't retired…yet. There's still time for him to make decisions without involving Pierce.

"No, but does he really have to know?"

I give him my best puppy eyes. It's the look he's never been able to say not to, and I hope like hell it works now. When he doesn't say anything, I try to make my eyes sadder. Probably not as cute as it was when I was eight, but hopefully it's enough.

"Fine." He shakes his head. "You have my blessing. But…if he finds out, it was your decision and I had nothing to do with it."

"You're still the boss, Dad. He can't order you around."

He puts an arm around my shoulder and gives me a small squeeze. "You think I don't know that? I don't want to undermine him, either. He'll be taking over the winery with all of you. The only reason he's in charge is because he's the oldest. But each and every one of you has equal say. Those are the rules."

"Does Pierce know? I think he might be a bit mixed up on your request."

"He'll grow out of it." Dad walks me to the door. "Don't be so hard on him, he's trying to figure it out like the rest of you. He just needs to find his groove."

"If you say so." I roll my eyes. "He has a funny way of doing it."

"Things will work out and he'll calm down. I was the same way when I took over from grandpa."

"Yeah, but you didn't have a million siblings."

"You don't either," he laughs. "There are only six of you, and Paula doesn't want anything to do with it. All of you will find your place with your strengths. It'll take each one of you to make this place run like a well-oiled machine."

He's not wrong. Each of us has something we're good at, but I don't think all of us will realize it until we give each other the chance to.

"I guess I see what you're saying." I open the door. "Hopefully it doesn't take as long as I fear it might for us to figure it out."

"I have faith in you." He kisses the top of my head and let's go of me so I can leave. "Maybe me and Mom will see you at the carnival this weekend."

The last thing I want is to run into them while I'm still trying to figure out what to do about the Beau situation. "I'll see you later, Dad. Thanks for letting me know where the cards are."

The amount of faith he has in us always amazes me. All of us are completely different and fought most of the time growing up. It was never serious, but I'm honestly surprised my brothers are as close as they are now. I guess getting older changes things. Well, most things. I'm still the baby and they take every opportunity to remind me of that.

Heat slams into me once I'm off my parents' porch. Yep, I definitely should have driven over here. But the walk back to the office gives me a chance to figure out what I'm wearing to the carnival. Of course, I want the outfit to be cute, but I also need to look professional if I'm handing out cards.

I don't think I've ever put this much thought into something I'm wearing to hang out with Beau. Impressing him has never been at the top of my thoughts, even though I've loved him for half of my life. This time it feels different, though. Something about this weekend feels like everything is about to change.

fourteen

· · ·

beau

NERVES RACE up my spine as I pull into Piper's driveway. You can't even tell there was a storm recently. She's even planted flowers in front of her house. Who knows where she got the time to do it. She's either at the winery, with me, or...on dates. Hopefully after tonight, that last one won't be something she's doing anymore. All of my fingers and toes are crossed.

The curtain in the window shifts. Is she watching out for me? That's new. Usually, I get here and walk right in. She's almost never ready for anything we have planned. I've made it a habit to tell her we need to be at a location slightly earlier than we need to be.

I put the car in park and open the door to see if she's ready. Before I can take a step, she's already walking down the sidewalk. Her hair is up in a ponytail that bounces every time she takes a step. I half expected her to be in a pair of leggings, but she has on shorts and a flowy top.

This is not the norm for her. Anytime we go to town functions she's usually sporting a t-shirt and leggings. Hell, she doesn't even wear makeup most of the time. Today is different. I need to figure out why.

"Did you forget how to say hello?" She waves at me as if she's not the only thing in the universe I focus on.

"Sorry. It's just." I wave my hand up and down over her outfit. "This is different. You don't even have on a ball cap."

"Occasionally I do dress like a functioning adult."

I move around the car to open the door for her before she makes it over here. "I know that." I wait until she's seated with her small bag in her lap before leaning in. "It's just not your usual outfit for a day of getting on rides and eating junk food."

She only shrugs instead of answering my unasked question. Fine, if she wants to be mysterious, I'll play along.

The parking spaces around the square are full. Dang, people got here early today. It's not even lunch, and families are already milling around booths. Maybe they want to get the school stuff out of the way before they let their kids loose on the rides. I don't blame them.

"Looks like we'll have to walk a bit." I turn toward one of the stores that's okay with people parking in their lot during town events. "I guess I underestimated how many people would be here this early."

"Pfft. Some people have already come and gone. It gets way too hot out here."

"What if their kids want to hang out at the carnival?" We were always here early and late as teens because we'd help some of our favorite teachers set up their booths for extracurricular activities. That never crossed my mind.

It might also be because I came with the Summers every year, too. My parents would give me money in case I wanted anything, but they never showed up to anything except graduation.

"They'll probably bring them back tonight once it cools off."

She has a point. It way too hot to be outside all day long. I'm pretty sure the city has put up tents with mist sprays. At least, I vaguely remember them doing that when I was a kid.

I park the car as close as I can to the square. We still have to walk almost a mile. I guess it's a good thing Piper wore a pair of tennis shoes today instead of heels or flip flops.

"Are you ready for this?" I ask after I open the passenger side door.

She slides the long strap of her bag over her head so that it hangs across the front of her. "As ready as I'll ever be."

We walk side by side down toward the festivities. Is she walking closer to me? We've always entered areas like this, but I swear I just felt her shoulder brush against mine. I know I shouldn't read too much into it, but maybe she's finally starting to show she has more than friendly feelings toward me. Keeping my cool until I get the courage to tell her how I feel is going to be difficult.

Groups of people are hanging out in various areas. Families are clustered around the school booths. It's nice seeing the community together. Even if these types of fairs happen at least once every three months. It's not something I saw in the town I lived in before I moved here as a kid.

I grunt as I get elbowed in my side. At first, I think it's a kid running by, but Piper is digging in her bag for something and not paying attention to where her arms are moving.

"Sorry." She winces as she finds what she's looking for and pulls it out. "I should have gotten these out before we got out of the car. I didn't realize how many people I would need to dodge."

"What are those?"

Her cheeks turn red, and I don't know if it's from the heat or embarrassment. "Business cards. I talked with the city manager, and he said it was okay for me to hand them out."

"Oh, I didn't realize we were doing marketing things today." My words are low and I'm almost certain I mumbled them. Disappointment courses through me. I thought we were going to have a fun day out. Something to make us feel like we were kids again, and completely unrelated to work. At least for a few hours.

"I figured it was a good idea. And it's technically free since the cards were in a box, buried behind a bunch of files." She stops and grabs my arm, noticing the change in my mood. She's the only person who knows how to read the subtle shifts. "I'm not handing them out all day."

"It's fine, and not a terrible idea. Though most of the people here already know about Starlit Fields."

"That's what Dad said, too. But there may be new folks in town."

She's not wrong. Our small town is rapidly growing, and I worry we'll lose the charm I've come to love.

We spend the next few hours passing out cards to over-worked, and overstimulated, parents. They gladly take them with the promise of a slow pace and good wine. I know for a fact some of these folks have been to the winery, but they need the reminder that it's okay for them to take some time to themselves.

With our hands now empty, we take in the food trucks, games, and rides.

"So, should we eat?" I grab her hand and pull her toward a trailer with corn roasting over an open fire and get in line.

"Yes, I'm starving. I didn't eat anything before you picked me up."

"Why not?" I know her, and she's not one to skip meals unless she's nervous. Talking to people comes easily to her though. If she planned to hand out cards today, she knew she was going to be sweet talking folks.

"Nerves, I guess." She glances at her hand still in mine, but she doesn't remove it. "I want to bring more business to the winery, and if the things we're doing don't work, I don't know what will happen going forward."

"It'll work, I promise." We're almost to the front and I glance to see if they have anything else. The board lists corn and drinks. There is a table off to the side with various condiments to add to the corn. "Just one? Do you want anything to drink?"

"One is fine. And water, please. It's too hot out here not to stay hydrated."

She's not lying. My shirt is damp from all the walking and I could use some water, too.

I place our order and once we have the roasted corn in our hands and fixed up the way we like, I search for a shaded area to sit. All the tables are full and I spot an open space under a tree. We'll have to sit on the ground, but I know she won't have an issue with it.

"It feels good to sit down." She says as she plops to the ground. "We haven't even been here that long and my feet are killing me."

"Maybe we should add some cardio to our marketing meetings."

"You're so funny." She bumps into me before taking a bit of the corn. "This is so good."

The moan that comes from her is more than I can handle, and I need a change of subject.

"So, you never told me. How was your date?"

It's the last thing I want to bring up, but I'm curious. She usually tells me how horrible her dates are, but this time she's been oddly quiet about it. Fear that it went well and is progressing to another date stabs me in the stomach. Maybe I'm not so hungry after all.

"It was fine." She shrugs her shoulders. "Rob took me bowling."

Rob? "Oh, so you're telling me their names now. It must be serious."

Another shrug. She's doing everything she can to keep her eyes off me. "He asked me on a second date."

"What did you say?" Please let the answer be no. She's gone on a couple of second dates that haven't gone anywhere. I shouldn't worry.

"I haven't answered him." She finishes off her corn, and I've barely touched mine. "Let's play some games. I think most of them are put on by school organizations and the profit is going toward their funds."

"Let's give these kids some money." I'm grateful for the change of subject and activity. As much as I tell her I'm okay with listening to her dating shenanigans, I don't know if I can stomach hearing about a date that went well enough for her to consider a second one.

"I cannot believe you talked me into getting on that death trap." Piper clings to my arm as we step off the ferris wheel.

This right here is exactly why I suggested it. She is terrified of heights, but always willing to go on this ride with me because she knows it's one of my favorites. It's the one ride that slows everything down and you're able to relax without a care in the world. Unless you're Piper, of course.

"You could have said no." I laugh. "It's not like I forced you onto it."

"I know, but I don't see why you like it so much. You can get the same feeling down here with both feet on the ground."

"Because you can't see the skyline from down here."

"Okay, you've got me there." She reaches for my hand and pulls me in the opposite direction. "Now you get to go in the funhouse with me."

It was the one concession I made for her. I'm not scared of funhouses, but sometimes they are too cramped and make me feel like I can't get out. Like the walls are closing in on me. It's not my favorite feeling in the world. Especially since it's how I felt my entire childhood having to tiptoe around my parents.

"Ten tickets," the person running the funhouse announces as we approach. "Each." He adds at the last minute.

"We should have gotten the wristbands," I mutter under my breath.

"Probably," Piper laughs and nudges me with her elbow.

I count out the twenty tickets and hand them over before taking the steps into my own personal nightmare.

"Do you think this is the same one they had out here when we were kids?" My steps are careful as we make our way over what feels like plywood to the first room.

"I doubt it. That thing was falling apart back then. I'm positive this is a new one."

"If you say so."

I follow her through each room, my hand never leaving hers. The one with stripes going in every direction always makes me sick to my stomach. It's too much chaos and reminds me of the times my parents would argue after they thought I was in bed.

I can see reflections as we enter the next room. Mirrors cover every wall and the hallways splits into multiple directions. Why did they have to make this is a maze?

Though this could work to my advantage. If we get stuck in a corner and don't have anywhere to go, she has to hear me out. This is my last chance or I'm going to chicken out the way I always do.

We turn left, then right, and another right. Honestly, seeing ourselves in every direction is disorienting. It's definitely not a space you can hide from yourself. Everything is on full display whether you like it or not.

"Shit, we hit a dead end," Piper says loud enough to be heard over the music blasting through the speakers. She turns around and slams into my chest. "Sorry, I didn't realize you were so close. We should turn around. I know how much you hate this attraction."

How convenient. She said the one thing I want to talk to her about. I walk her backwards until she's between me and one of these God forsaken mirrors. Focus Beau.

"What are you doing?" She glances up at me. "You hate this place."

"I want to talk to you." Honestly, the ferris wheel would have been a better place because there was absolutely nowhere to go. I guess the best part is if things don't go the way I'm hoping, we can leave easier.

"A-about what?" Her voice is soft and barely above a whisper. Our close proximity is the only reason I can hear her.

"My feelings toward you." She opens her mouth to respond, but I cut her off. "Look, I know you think that night was a fluke. That I only kissed you back because I was in shock. But, Piper, that couldn't be further from the truth. I've wanted to taste your lips since we were teenagers."

"No." She shakes her head and tries to head back down the hallway, but stops when my hand meets the mirror, blocking her escape. "You're just trying to make me feel better."

"I'm really not, Piper."

"Yes, you are. We've been best friends for years, you're just confusing the emotions."

There she goes again trying to write off the connection between us. "What can I do to prove it to you?"

She's looking around trying to figure out how she should answer this question. A war raging inside her head. Finally, she smirks because she's come to a decision and it's one she doesn't think I'll follow through with.

"Kiss me."

She's wrong. My lip crash into hers with zero hesitation.

fifteen

. . .

piper

HOLY SHIT. It's the first thought that runs through my mind when his mouth meets mine. He actually did it. I didn't think he would. Probably not smart on my part. Telling him to kiss me was like waving a big flag daring him to do it. What the hell was I thinking? Easy, I wasn't.

It doesn't take me long to ignore every thought running through my head about it being a bad idea. Deep down, I knew him acting on the request would answer my question about how he felt about it.

The mirror is the only thing holding me up at this point, and I hope like hell it's strong because he leans closer into me. It's not until I realize his arm is wrapped around my waist that we're no longer holding hands. When did that happen?

Worrying about that right now isn't something I need to do. Not when I'm in his arms as more than a friendly hug, or cuddle. No, the way his body is pressed against mine, and I can feel him through his jeans, tells me everything I need to know.

I open one eye and can't stop from moaning in his mouth. In the mirror opposite us, I can see everything, and damn, I didn't think I'd find that a turn on. Him pressed against me, and I can't go anywhere. Not that I want to, but the visual will keep me up for nights. I squeeze my eyes shut to keep me in the moment.

My arms snake around his neck and pull him closer, deepening the kiss. He tastes like the cotton candy we shared earlier, and nothing has ever tasted so sweet.

His hand slides into my back pocket, finding any way he can to envelope every part of my body.

He pulls away and I miss the feel of his lips on mine. He whispers in my ear, his lips a soft touch. "Is that proof enough?"

All I can do is nod. My voice finally comes back to me. "Yes. I was, uh, actually going to tell you I have feelings for you, but I chickened out."

He leans his forehead against mine. "Why didn't you say something instead of making me prove it to you?"

"It was the only way I could think of to make sure I was reading the situation right." I shrug and look down.

He slides a finger under my chin and lifts until my eyes meet his. "You never have to play games with me." He kisses the tip of my nose. "I've been yours." A kiss on the cheek. "Since we were thirteen."

He lips meet mine once again. He's taking his time making sure his actions hold meaning. I love him for that, but I've waited so long for this, and I'm done being patient.

My tongue traces a line along the seam of his lips and

he opens wider. Our tongues dancing. He's no longer blocking my exit, and with both hands under my ass, lifts me until him and the wall are the only things holding me up.

I cling to him. Not because I'm afraid I'll fall, but because I worry, he'll come to his senses and pull away. His mouth leaves mine and he trails kisses down my neck. Chancing another peek over his shoulder and this may be the hottest thing I've ever seen or done. Mirrors in my room are an investment I need to make.

Right now, we're like teenagers without a care in the world. Living in our own bubble nothing else can penetrate.

The music switches to another song and I swear I hear mumbling coming from the entrance. Beau doesn't seem to hear anything because he's gone from kissing my neck to my chest, making his way to the other side.

"Mom," a kid's voice breaks through the music. I knew I heard something.

"Did you hear that?" My voice is a whisper in the overly loud space. I don't think he can hear me because he only leans in closer, marking every spot of me he can reach.

A thud sounds in the distance this time. I tap on Beau's shoulder until I have his attention and his face is level with mine again. "I think someone is coming."

"How can you tell? It's so loud in here." He leans into me, pressing my back harder against the mirror.

As his mouth moves closer to mine, I see a shoe out of the corner of my eye. I drop my legs and push Beau away from me. Not hard, but enough to let him know we aren't alone.

Beau runs a hand through his hair in an attempt to tame it. I really wish he wouldn't. A kid comes all the way into view. "Sorry, kid, this is a dead end."

"Thanks." The child waves and heads back in the direction he came.

"That was a close call." I do my best to make sure my clothes are straightened out. The last thing I want to do is walk out of here looking like a hot mess.

"Yeah." He glances toward the opening before giving me one last kiss. "Wanna get out of here?"

"I thought you'd never ask." I grab his hand and lead him out of the hall.

"What's your rush?"

"What do you think?" I glance back to make sure he's following me. He is, but his eyes are on my ass. Has he always done that and I've never noticed? It's possible. All this time I thought he didn't feel anything for me. Most people aren't that oblivious, except me.

"I agree, though funhouses may be my new favorite attraction at these fairs."

Those are words I never thought I'd hear him say. "Oh yeah?"

"Yep." I can feel him move closer to me. "It's now where we shared our first real kiss."

"Technically that was at your house."

"That doesn't count." He stops me before I can take another step. "We didn't know what we do now. It makes all the difference."

If he keeps saying things like that, we'll never make it out of here. "Why are there so many freaking hallways? This place doesn't look that big from the outside."

"It's not." He steps in front of me and tilts his head to

the side. "That sounds like laughter. I bet we can find our way out of here if we follow it."

"Lead the way." It's probably the kid from a few minutes ago. But I'll do anything to get out of this attraction and fair. I no longer feel like being here. There are other things I'd rather be doing.

A few moments later we're climbing stairs, walking across a bridge that looks like it's tilted, and I can see the lights from a ride in the short distance. We're almost there.

As soon as we get close to the exit, bubbles pour out of the doorway. We're covered from head to toe, laughing at the ridiculousness of it all. I don't remember bubbles when we were kids. It must be something new.

Beau pulls me into his arms and kisses me…in front of everyone. He has no qualms about letting the world know how he feels. When he pulls back, he has the biggest smile I've seen on him since we graduated high school. "Your place or mine?"

"Definitely yours. It's closer."

"Good choice." He moves his hand to mine and interlocks our fingers. This feels right. Even the few times I've held hands with dates, it never felt like this. Like us against the world. It's nice knowing I have someone in my corner. Even better, he knows me inside and out.

I guess he was right that night on his couch. There's something between us, and if I'm honest, it's been there since we were young. I was too busy doing everything I could to bury those feelings so I wouldn't screw up anything. That's probably not a healthy way to deal with emotions, but I didn't want to put a wedge in our friendship. Other than my siblings, he's the only person I trust completely. Here's to hoping things go well with us.

The drive to Beau's house is quiet. Neither of us wants to break the easy silence we're sharing. Both of us are probably running a million different scenarios through our heads.

Despite that, the energy buzzing throughout the car is palpable. Every part of me wants to touch him. Kiss him and mark him as mine...finally.

We pull into his driveway in record time. I'm pretty sure he broke some speed limit laws to get us here as fast as possible. As soon as the car is in park and turned off, he rushes around to my side of the car and pulls the door open. It's one of my favorite things about him. He's always such a gentleman. Except back in the funhouse. I've never seen that side of him.

Before he has a chance to close the door behind me, I'm wrapping my arms around his neck. The need to be close to him is overwhelming, but I'm going with the flow, and this feels right.

I walk him backwards, and he closes the car door with a quick kick. He trips as we continue the path to his front door, and we both almost fall.

"Maybe we should get inside first." He laughs as he straightens us back up. "Otherwise, we might end up breaking something and that would be a less fun ending to the night."

"Fine," I pout. He's right. It's dark out here since he didn't turn on the porch light. I don't think he realized how long we'd be gone. If I'm being honest, I didn't think we'd stay until after dark either. We were having fun, though. There was no reason to cut the evening short.

He fishes his keys out of his pocket and quickly unlocks the door. He pulls me in as soon as it's open and slams it shut behind us. "Now, where were we?"

My arms go around his neck and he lifts me up until my legs wrap around his waist. Good. The last thing I want to do is trip over something in his hallway. It takes us less than a minute to get to his bedroom.

It's dark aside from the soft glow of his alarm clock. I've been in here hundreds of times, but tonight is different and will shift everything between us. For once, I'm no longer thinking with my head and relying solely on my heart. If it comes back to bite me in the ass, so be it.

He lays me down on the bed without a word. The action so sweet and meticulous unlike the way I practically attacked him in the driveway.

"We can stop now, if you want." His words are loud in his quiet house, even though it's barely a whisper.

"I-I don't want to stop." We can figure out relationship stuff tomorrow. Tonight, I want to be wrapped in his arms and feel him all over me.

"Okay." He reaches for my shorts, slowly undoing the button and zipper. Shivers course through my body at the sensation as he slides them down. Never in my wildest dreams did I think this would happen between us. Harboring a crush for my best friend for over a decade and nothing happen, makes this moment that much more special.

Once my shorts and panties are off, he places soft kisses along my thighs. Now more than ever, I wish he'd stop being so careful and sweet. It's one of the things I love about him, but I need him to pick up the pace.

I prop myself up on my elbows and watch as his tongue swirls around my clit and a finger slips inside. He doesn't have to worry about how ready I am because I have been since he pinned me against the mirror in the funhouse. I fall back as he goes deeper.

Normally, I'm the type of person to take control in the bedroom, but I feel safe with Beau. He has always been my sanctuary and being intimate with him is no different.

His tongue moves faster and his finger matches the pace. My body lifts the closer I am to release, and his free hand slides over my waist to hold me down. The sensation is too much and before long I'm biting back a scream.

He leans back with a smug smirk on his face. Yes, he was right about the chemistry between us and that I had feelings about him, but damn…he doesn't have to look so happy about it.

It takes him less than a minute to stand and strip away his clothes. "Is this still, okay?"

"Mhmm." It's all I can manage right now. My shirt gets stuck in my hair as I try to pull it off while lying down.

Beau reaches over me and it sounds like a drawer is sliding over. I hear the foil rip and I'm glad he's at least prepared. I know I'm sure as hell not.

"You have no idea how long I've wanted you." His lips crash into mine. Moments later, I feel him enter me as he deepens this kiss. Little does he know I've probably wanted him just as long.

Our bodies move in sync as if this is the way it's always supposed to have been. I can tell he's close, but he's waiting for me to tip over the edge. He slides a hand between us, rubbing my clit with his thumb and that's all the encouragement I need.

I cling to him as if my very being depends on it as wave after wave of pleasure courses through my body. He follows shortly after.

He doesn't fall on top of me the way some men I've been with do. Instead, he slowly pulls out before standing. "Give me just a sec, I'll be right back."

I watch as he heads toward the bathroom. He's gone for a couple of minutes before coming back. He has a towel in his hand and instead of handing it to me, he cleans me up. The towel is warm and damp.

Clearly, I've been dating the wrong guys in my life. I'm lucky if they even hand me a towel most of the time.

"Thanks." I whisper into the quiet room.

"If you want to take a shower, you know where every-thing is." His smile is soft and unsure this time. Afraid I'm going to bolt now that the adrenaline has worn off.

"I'm good. But give me a few minutes." I grab a blanket he keeps on a chair by his bed and wrap myself in it. There's no way in hell I'm leaving.

Everything about tonight was perfect, and forced me to act on my feelings. If he hadn't said anything, I would have kept pretending like I only saw him as a friend. But he did, and that led us to now. This moment will forever alter our relationship.

sixteen

. . .

beau

DID LAST NIGHT REALLY HAPPEN? It all feels like a fever dream. Piper lying next to me and cutting off the circulation in my arm proves everything was real. She kissed me back, and told me she has feelings for me. A part of me wonders how long she's had them, but the bigger part of me doesn't give a damn. All that matters is she's in my arms right now.

I need to go to the restroom, but I don't want to wake up Piper. She needs the sleep. The thought she might bolt wiggles its way into my head, and I kick that idea to the curb. She would have done that last night if she was going to. At least, I think that's what would have happened.

For once I'm cursing my blackout curtains. I know she would look ethereal in the early morning light. Maybe one day I'll see it.

Closing my eyes, I cuddle her and do my best to drift

back to sleep. Who knows how long this will last, and I want to savor it.

A shrill ring sounds around the room and I jump up. Piper pulls me back down. "Ignore it."

"What is that?"

"My phone. It's the ring tone set for all my siblings." She grumbles into the pillow.

"I've been with you when they've called, and it's never made that sound before."

She wraps an arm around my waist and rests her head on my chest. "That's before they did shit to piss me off. Now I like to have a warning system for when they call. It lets me know who's calling before I even answer. Most of the time I ignore it. The only person who has a different one is Paula because right now, she's my favorite."

"It's so weird you have favorites and it depends on who you're mad at." Another thing I'll never relate to. Well, I guess I do in some aspect because her family treats me like I belong to them.

"If you had siblings, you'd understand." She rolls over and I think she's staring at the ceiling, but I can't tell. Damn these curtains.

The room is silent now that the phone has stopped ringing, and both of us are taking everything in. I have questions, but I'm scared of the answers. It's the only thing holding me back from asking them.

"Do we really have to get out of bed and adult today?" Piper groans before coming back to my side. This is a move in the right direction.

"Not really." I pull her closer. "It's Sunday and neither of us have anything we have to do…unless your brother is about to pile more work on you. As far as I'm concerned, we can stay in bed all day."

"I don't know about all that." Piper laughs. "I do need to be somewhat productive."

"What did you have in mind?" I hope it involves more of last night's activities, but I have a feeling she's going to burst my little happy bubble.

"I'd like to get some images and video for the social channels." She looks up at me and the realization that we're here right now…together, hit's me in the chest. "If that's okay with you. But I'll need your help."

Why hasn't this woman figured out I would do literally anything for her. All she has to do is ask.

"Sure. But maybe we can start with breakfast."

Her stomach growls as soon as the words leave my mouth. We ate an early dinner yesterday, but nothing after the ferris wheel.

"That's probably a good idea." She moves away and grabs the blanket she used last night to wrap around her. "Do you have anything I can wear? I don't feel like putting yesterday's clothes on again."

"Sweatpants are in the bottom drawer, and I think I have some t-shirts in the top drawer." It's not like she can see anything, though. I slide out of bed and pull on the jeans I discarded last night before turning on the light.

This is the view I wanted as soon as I woke up. Piper's hair disheveled and her wrapped up in me. Too bad right now she's all the way across the room.

"I'll be out to help you in a few minutes." She opens the drawer looking through my shirts. I have no idea what's in there. Most of them I throw on to do yard work without a second thought.

"Take your time." My eyes slide over her one more time before I head to the guest bathroom. Brushing my teeth is at the top of my priority list right now. Especially if I hope to kiss her this morning.

And I know my friend enough to know she needs time to herself in the morning. One of the side effects of having so many people in the house growing up.

Five minutes later I'm in the kitchen pulling ingredients out of the fridge. I hope like hell I have everything I need for breakfast. Getting groceries has been low on my priority list lately and it shows. Luckily, I find some bacon. Piper isn't a huge fan of eggs, and I rummage through my pantry for the pancake mix I bought not too long ago when I was craving them.

Mostly, I'm trying to get most of the cooking done before Piper comes in the kitchen. As much as she wants to help, we both know she's not great with cooking. It's the main reason I bring her food whenever I can. Otherwise, I don't know if she's eating anything other than frozen dinners.

I grab a skillet from the cabinet and put it on the stove to preheat while I get a bowl down to mix the pancake batter. By the time I hear her footsteps coming into the kitchen, the bacon is sizzling and I'm almost ready to pour the batter.

"What can I help with?"

"I've got it, just sit at the table," I call out over my shoulder not wanting to spill anything.

When I turn around, she's standing behind me. My sweatpants are baggy on her and she's wearing a shirt I've had since high school. It was to support one of the playoff games and it hangs loose on her. Not going to lie, seeing her in my clothes does something to me. It's not the first time she's worn something of mine, but after yesterday, it means something different.

She's mine, or at least I hope she is. We still need to have that conversation. But for now, I'll enjoy the view of her being in my clothes.

"Why are you staring at me?" She messes with her hair and turns to the microwave to check her reflection. "Do I have something on my face?"

Of course, she would feel self-conscious when I'm looking at her. Though maybe she really thinks she has something on her face.

"No." I shake my head and walk toward her. My arms wrap around her waist, pulling her to me. "You look fucking perfect."

She laughs and smacks my arm. "I look like I just rolled out of bed, which I did."

"True, but that doesn't mean you aren't perfect."

"Please, don't act like you haven't seen me like this before."

"I have." I bend down, placing a kiss on her forehead. "But." A kiss to the tip of her nose. "Now." Another to her cheek. "I can do this."

I capture her lips with mine and she doesn't hesitate parting her lips to deepen the kiss. Her fingers dig into my back as I lift her up and set her on the counter. Her legs wrap around me, pulling me closer to her. There's no way in hell she can't feel my erection against her.

She tries to pull away, but my hands gripping her waist don't let her move back. A bite to my bottom lip has me pulling up short, unsure if that's something I like or not.

The look on her face has me dropping the line of thought. Her nose is scrunched up.

"What's wrong?"

She points toward the stove. "You're burning the food."

"Oh shit." I release my hold on her and slip from between her legs, rushing to turn off the burners.

Laughter is all I can hear as I try to scrape the now burnt food onto a plate. "I guess now you can't give me shit about not being able to cook."

"That's not fair." I set the skillet in the sink and run a hand though my hair. "I was distracted."

"Oh no." She waves her hand in front of her. "I'm not taking the blame for this. That is all you. You decided to kiss me. I only responded."

"As if I could resist that," I mutter.

She must have heard me because she snorts. "Get dressed. We'll run through a drive through and we can go to my house."

"You're awfully bossy this morning." I stare at the skillet hoping I didn't ruin it. I don't think I did. Even if it is, it was worth it. I would ruin every dish I own if it meant having her in my arms.

"Not really. I'm just on the verge of hangry and we both know we don't want that to happen."

She's not wrong. The meanness that comes out of her when she's hungry isn't something anyone should experience.

"Okay," I sigh. Looks like this mess will have to wait until later to get cleaned up. "Give me five minutes."

"You have two."

There's no use arguing with her. Knowing her, she's timing me and she'll take my car whether or not I'm ready. She's done it in the past when we would go to parties and I didn't get to the car fast enough.

I rush to my room, change jeans and throw on a plain black t-shirt before slipping on my shoes. It's a good thing I took care of my teeth and hair earlier. The failed breakfast attempt is cleared away, aside from the dishes, when I come back to the kitchen.

"Wow, that was record time." Piper grins as she comes toward me and pats me on the cheek. She knows I hate it, but she doesn't mean anything by it. "Let's get some food in our bellies."

Reaching for my hand, she interlocks our fingers and pulls me toward the front door. I have just enough frame of mind to grab my keys from the counter. One day she'll realize she doesn't have to coerce me into doing what she wants. All she has to do is ask.

Why is Piper's house always so damn cold? I grab one of the hoodies I left out of her closet and throw it over my head. These things should not be worn in the middle of August, but here we are.

She's in the living room waiting for me to sit down so we can eat. "Finally," she sighs as I take the spot next to her.

Most people would think we're weird because we have specific places we sit on the couch. She has her cushion and I have mine. Her siblings always say we act like a married couple. Kind of hard not to after a decade long friendship. Though this morning, both of us are much closer to each other than normal.

There's no hesitation as she digs into her breakfast. She wasn't lying when she said she was on the verge of hangry. How many other people would make sure she gets food when she needs it? Nobody is the answer…except me. I doubt Rob would.

I should wait until we're done eating to ask, but if I don't ask now, I never will. "Sooo, where do we go from here?"

She swallows the bite she took and turns her head toward me. "What do you mean?"

Of course, she's playing like she doesn't know exactly what I'm asking.

"Us? Are we staying friends? Or, are we going to give dating a real shot?"

Her fork hits her plate with a clatter. Oh shit. I fucked up. Leaning back, she crosses her arms over her chest. All it does is make me notice she still hasn't changed out of my clothes, and that eases my mind…slightly.

"After last night, and the burnt food this morning, I'm surprised you even have to ask."

My shoulders loosen and I breathe a sigh of relief. "I just wanted to make sure because yesterday you were talking about a possible date with that guy. I don't want to pressure you into anything."

"When have I ever let anyone affect what I do?" She has a point. "Besides Rob doesn't hold a candle to you. I truly want to see if we can make a relationship work. If things get weird, we can always go back to our bestie dynamic."

The surety in her voice washes away any doubt I have

about how she feels toward me. Before I realize it, her lips are on mine, much like that night at my house. Only this time I can taste the sweet maple from the syrup on her pancakes. All thoughts of breakfast are gone. There's only me and her.

seventeen

. . .

piper

WHY DO I have to be at work right now instead of hanging out with Beau? I mean, I've always preferred being with him instead of work, but now I definitely want to do that more often. Not even because we're pretty damn compatible in bed, but it's nice holding his hand and cozying up to him in ways I never thought possible. Maybe I should have relayed how I felt sooner.

Peter's voice startles me. "Do you have those reports for Pierce?"

Gah, I need to stop daydreaming about my best friend and do my job. "Which ones?" There were a couple Pierce asked me to run. He's gonna need to be a little more specific.

He narrows his eyes and he looks so much like our eldest brother it makes me want to smack him. I don't know why he tries to emulate him so much. Pierce is kind of an asshole and that shouldn't be anyone's goal.

"The list of wines that have been selling in the last three weeks." Ugh, even his tone is the same. Someone really needs to tell these older Summers' kids they'll get things done faster if they are nicer. Would it be immature of me to tell Dad? Probably. But our parents are the only people they listen to.

I shuffle through the stack of papers on my desk and pull it out, pausing before I hand it to him. "You know, it's polite to say please."

He rolls his eyes. "May I please have the reports?"

The way we all use sarcasm toward each other should be studied. His "please" is exaggerated and isn't doing him any favors with me. If I don't give him the reports, he's likely to stay in my office for longer than I want him to.

"Fine," I mumble and hand them over. "Is there anything else the all-mighty Pierce needs?"

"A girlfriend," Peter laughs. It's not the response I was expecting. Usually, he gets mad when the rest of us mock our big brother. My second oldest brother has managed to render me speechless. Not something that happens often.

"You haven't noticed how grouchy he's been? It's like one minor inconvenience sets him off."

"As opposed to when? That seems to be his status quo with the rest of us who don't worship the ground he walks on." My voice has returned and I have a feeling he'll report what I'm saying to Pierce, but I don't really care. It's not anything I haven't said to his face at some point.

"That's not how—" He stops as soon as I hold up my finger. I know exactly how he was going to finish that sentence and there's no way he can deny his hero worship of our brother. "Look, I just want to make him and Dad proud."

"You can do that without being their lapdog." It's a low blow, and I know that as soon as the words are out of my mouth. Him and Philip are the middle children, but instead of doing whatever he wants, he tries to please everyone he sees in an authoritative position.

"Noted." He nods and leaves the office, shoulders sagging and head down.

Going after him is probably the right thing to do, but I know it won't amount to anything. Not while he's upset.

I'm such a shitty sister. Yes, I'm the baby but that doesn't mean I need to act like the world revolves around me. Stopping by his house this evening has moved up my priority list when I get off work. Sadly, that means I won't see Beau until later.

My phone dings with a text and I fully expect it to be Beau. He's pretty much the only person who messages me in the middle of the day. Except it's not him, it's...my sister.

PAULA

Lunch at Ashes. 2 hours.

Well, she's being demanding isn't she. Despite working for the family, I can't do whatever I want. I have to see if anyone needs my help with anything. Before I have a chance to reply, my phone dings again.

PAULA

Don't bother coming up with a reason why you can't meet me. If you don't show up, I'll be forced to come to the winery.

She acts like that is such a hardship. She washed her hands of the business years ago, aside from an event here or there.

PIPER

> I'll be there. Don't get a seat at the bar. I don't need Eric all up in our business.

PAULA

> That's a given. See you soon baby sis.

She knows I hate when they call me that. It's true, but that isn't the only thing I am. When will they see I'm my own person?

There's nothing I can do about it. No use dwelling over what my older siblings call me. There's work to do and I need to get these orders over to Pierce if I want them to go out today.

He's doing inventory wine when I walk into the temperature-controlled warehouse. Every time I come in here, he's counting bottles. Does he think they are going missing?

After a quick glance, I notice the bottles that were there a week ago are dwindling. Looks like all my efforts are paying off.

"We have more orders," I announce cheerfully.

He jumps and bumps his head on the shelf above him. I do everything in my power not to giggle. Catching the big brother unaware is a hard feat and yet, I've managed it.

"Do I have a bump?" He leans his head toward me, rubbing the spot he hit.

I set the papers on the shelf and lean over him. "You know, I'd be able to see better if you moved your hand."

"Sorry." It's a soft mumble as I push his hair aside and feel around the area his hand vacated seconds ago.

"I don't feel anything." Grabbing the papers, I hold them out to him. "Now, if you're done being a baby, here are the new orders that came in."

"Did you get those other reports to Peter?"

"Yep. What does he need them for anyway?"

"He's seeing which wines are selling the most so we know what we need to keep on hand. The sales have been blowing up after the past couple of days. We've even had more people walk in according to Parker."

The urge to tell him it's because of me floods through every vein in my body. I can't though. He's not supposed to know I'm doing the exact opposite of what he said.

"That's good." I glance toward the shipping area. We have to be careful with online orders because there are only certain places we can even ship to. "Are those all the boxes we have left?"

"Yeah, I need to order some more."

"Can we please update the design? Those look so outdated." They haven't been changed since my grandpa was running the winery, and you can tell.

He studies them for a moment, and glances at the wine. "Do you have something in mind?"

Not really, but I will if he gives me the okay. "I can come up with something."

Another few moments pass. He's going to tell me no, I just know it. "Fine, you can do the design for the boxes. But before you send them to Peter to order, I want to make sure it aligns with the brand."

As if I'd ever do anything to muck up our winery

brand. "Sure thing. What's Philip up to? I haven't seen him around."

"He's bottling more wine. We're selling the sangria almost as fast as he gets the bottles done."

My smirk is small, barely noticeable. At least, I hope. Those sales are one hundred percent because of me. I'm considering that a win. We haven't even put out all the content Beau has planned with me. It's good to know the videos we have done are working.

"Do you need help getting the orders out?" The list is kind of long, but with both of us we can get it knocked out pretty quickly. "I can help you for a bit before I have to meet Paula for lunch."

"Why do you have to?" He tilts his head to the side like a confused puppy.

"Because she ordered me to. You know I can't say no to the big sister."

"But you say no to me all the time. How is that fair?"

"She's nicer." I can say it with a straight face because it's the truth. She actually listens to me…unlike some people.

His only response is a grunt as he moves toward the shipping table. "I think I've got it. You can head out early if everything else is cleared up. You don't want to keep Paula waiting."

Shock. That's all I feel right now. He never lets me leave early. I mean, I do it anyway. What's the perk of being one of the future owners if I can't head out sometimes.

"Thanks." My feet are quick as I run up and hug him. His body is rigid. No doubt he's surprised. I rarely show this level of excitement towards him.

"Before you go, can you mark the sangria as low inventory on the site? I don't want to fill backorders if at all possible."

"You've got it." I give him a mock salute before rushing out of the warehouse. Can't take a chance on him changing his mind.

Paula is nowhere to be seen when I walk into Out of the Ashes. She's here because I saw her car, but I'm glad she's not at the bar. It's awesome to be listened to when I voice an opinion.

"She's at the table in the back corner." Eric calls from behind the counter. "Don't think because you're back there, I won't find out what's going on."

Good gravy. He's worse than the gossiping old ladies. "You can try." I grin and head to the back area of the bar.

As soon as I round the corner, I see my sister sitting at a high top with a menu in hand. She doesn't realize I'm here yet.

"There's no point in even looking at the thing. You get the same food every time." I wrap my arm around her shoulder giving her a quick squeeze before sitting across from her.

"You're one to talk." She sets the menu on the table and waves Lisa over as soon as she sees her.

We give her our order. Wings and a margarita for me. Grilled chicken salad and a glass of wine for Paula.

"So, you and Beau are finally an item."

"Where did you hear that?" Thank God she waited for

Lisa to walk off. We've been spending time together, but we haven't made a town announcement or anything.

"Girl, it was all over town Sunday morning." She glances around to make sure Eric isn't listening in. We both know he likes to dig his fingers into everyone's problems.

"How does anyone know anything?" I love my small town, but at the same time, it drives me bananas. None of these people can mind their own damned business.

"Did you really think you'd be able to kiss in public and nobody would talk about it?" She shakes her head. "Why do you think I made sure to be seen with Tristan before we went on the family vacation? I needed there to be proof outside of me saying he was my boyfriend."

"I didn't think anyone would be watching us under a microscope." Does Beau know we're the talk of the town?

"Please, nobody is paying that much attention to you. But when he practically claims you in the middle of a town fair. It's gonna be the top story."

She has a point. We should have waited until we got back to his place. It's not abnormal to see us together. It is to see him with his tongue down my throat. Even if we're gossip fodder, I don't regret it one bit. Then the words my sister first said to me hit me.

"Wait, what did you mean by finally?"

Instead of answering, she laughs. Not quietly or politely. No, her hand slaps the table, and I wonder if she's going to knock it over trying to keep herself in her chair.

"You're funny." She points to me as soon as she's able to calm down. "The two of you have been dancing around each other since you were thirteen. For whatever ridiculous reason everyone could see it, except both of you."

"I didn't think anyone could tell I had a crush on him. He never noticed."

"That's because you have four brothers and had no idea how to flirt that didn't involve punching." She shakes her head and tightens her ponytail. "Honestly, I probably should have stepped in when I realized you liked him as more than a friend."

"Eh, it was better that we figured it out on our own time. Though, I kind of feel bad for telling him about all my failed dates now."

Paula is shaking her head. "No, don't apologize for that. He didn't clue you in on how it made him feel so you didn't know." Lisa sets our drinks in front of us and then heads back to the kitchen. "Now, how did you make the first move?"

"I actually didn't." My cheeks burn relaying how everything went down. This is nice. Being able to talk to my sister about something good that doesn't involve bitching about our siblings is exactly what I needed today.

eighteen

. . .

beau

"BEAU, can you meet me in my office?" Mr. Gardner says as he walks past me. I'm not sure if this is a good thing or not. I can only assume he wants to talk to me about the progress on my marketing project with Piper.

Slowly I roll my chair back and stand. I don't miss the way Cole is staring at me. Maybe he thinks I'm in trouble. I could be. Who knows? There's only one way to find out.

My steps are slow as I make my way to his office. This feels so much like the first time I walked in here and he told me he wanted me to go ahead with the plan. He's already sitting behind his desk, and I close the door behind me as I enter. Might as well do that now in case he really is unhappy with the work I'm doing. None of it has interfered with my actual job. At least, for the most part. There are few things I run numbers on up here, but not much.

"How's the marketing plan going for your friend?" He

leans back and clasps his hands in front of his chest. Why does he keep doing that? It looks odd, and kind of like he doesn't know what to do with his hands.

"It's going well. We've been focusing mostly on social media. She also handed out business cards at a town festival."

"Did it work?"

I'm not sure which he's talking about. You can't really know the success when they are done in tandem.

"Which one?"

"Both. Unless you didn't separate them out." He cocks his head to the side as if I don't already know that.

"The social media posts are definitely working. She said online orders have seen a big uptick. I don't know the exact numbers, but she wouldn't tell me it's helped if it didn't."

"And the business cards?"

"I don't have data on that yet. We're supposed to meet tonight to go over a few things, plus the next step in our plan."

Everything I tell him is a piece of the truth. Pierce has been sending me actual numbers, and the progress has been pretty amazing. Honestly, Piper should be proud of herself. She's doing things for the winery nobody else has managed. It would be a lot better if Pierce would tell her he knows. As much as I want to, I can't be the one who breaks the news. Not only would she be incredibly pissed at me, but her brother would as well.

He leans forward, elbows on the desk, his hands still clasped but now they look like a steeple. Sort of like that song we learned in Sunday school. I'm not a fan of this pose either, but at least I seem to have gotten his interest again.

"Can you tell me a little about that?"

While I can't give him a ton of information, I can relay some of what I've discussed with Piper.

"She's mostly been using static posts and videos in her socials, but we're going to try going live. We have to be careful with the different platforms because of what they allow and don't. But we think it will be a good move."

He grins and leans back in his chair once again. "I've been hearing that from a lot of our clients. Making themselves available to their customers gives them an upper hand."

I don't know about upper hand. It does let people get to know you better. The more your audience connects with you, the more likely they are to support you in your business endeavors. Hell, it's how I've become a fan of some clothing companies and I'll always buy from them.

"We're working on some popup type events in the future, but I won't have data on those until we can get them scheduled."

"Sounds good. If you need any help, let me know." I stand and head toward the door. Being in this office with him is not my idea of a good time. "You're doing good work here. Keep it up and you'll be in one of the top spots here."

"Thank you, Sir."

Before he has a chance to offer any more wisdom, I hightail it out of his office. The last thing I want to do is be in a position of power at this place. If that ever happens, I'd much rather have my own firm. At least then I could work with companies I care about and not have to play the numbers game quite so hard.

Cole is already at my desk when I get there. "Drinks tonight?"

This guy always seems to want to go out after I get out of the boss's office. Yes, it's office politics, but I've never been one to play them.

"Sorry, taking my girlfriend out for dinner." Finally, I can say that. The rush of that one simple word on my tongue is enough to keep me from being too annoyed at the Cole.

"Cool. Well, if you change your mind, you know where we'll be." As if I would ever choose them over Piper. Girlfriend or not. "I'd love to pick your brain about what you're doing with your side project."

Of course he would. That's not going to happen. He has been handed everything since he started working here, and passes off all the actual work to other people. I refuse to be the one who lets him take advantage of me. Not that I don't believe in helping my coworker, but so many in the office have piled his stuff onto their desk, and it's not their job. Just because he's related to the boss doesn't mean he gets special treatment.

The end of the work day cannot come soon enough. Maybe it's not a bad idea to start thinking about doing my own thing. I'll see what Piper thinks. She's the only person I trust to tell me if it's a good idea or not.

Piper's door is unlocked...again. Maybe she should get one of those locks with an app. She's more likely to remember because it'll be on her phone. Other than me, the only people who really come to her house is her family. She has all packages delivered to the office because most of them won't go the extra half mile to take it to her house.

A problem I never had when I lived down the street. But I was with my parents back then. They've moved away since I graduated high school.

"Is that you, Beau?" Her voice is loud in the quiet house. It's shocking she doesn't have music playing. But I guess the tinkle of bells attached to the door let her know my presence.

I close the door behind me. It sounds like what I imagine glitter falling sounds like. Where did she even get these? We're not even close to Christmas.

"Why is your door not locked again?" Her voice came from her room and it's the first place I check. Except the room is empty.

"You are the only person coming today. I didn't see the point."

I follow her voice to the bathroom on the opposite side of the room. "I know you don't think anything will happen to you out here, especially with your family around. But...you never know."

"You worry way too much." She laughs. "How did you like my bells? It's practically a warning system for when I forget to lock the door."

"They are definitely loud. Did you have to search through the Christmas decor to find them?"

"Actually, I stole them off a wreath I found in the closet."

The wreath she's talking about comes to mind. She found it on the curb because someone was throwing it out. It's hideous, but she hung it on her door for the holiday season because I dared her to. She tried putting it on my door, but I shot down that idea as soon as she voiced it.

"I can't believe you still have that thing."

She shrugs as she applies her lipstick. "Me either. I actually forgot I had it until it fell after I moved a box."

This bit of information doesn't shock me. She always moves things around and unearths items from the past. Honestly, sometimes I wonder if her house isn't a time capsule. I'm pretty sure it would tell the history of our friendship.

Now she's putting on mascara. This is more than she's ever done when we've gone out to dinner. Not that it happens often. We like to get food and bring it home because we can drink cheaper on our couches.

"What's with all the makeup?" I hope like hell she doesn't take it the wrong way.

"We're going on a date?" Her statement comes out more like a question, and uncertainty flashes across her face.

"Yeah, but it's still just me." Not that I mind. I've seen her when she's dressed to the nines for a date. The last thing I want her to do is think she has to go through all this to impress me. She's been doing that since we were teenagers.

"It's still a date." She grins and her reflection in the mirror is breathtaking. "And I occasionally like to get dressed up. Believe me, it's not all about you."

"Okay then." I hold my hands up in surrender. She's not wrong. I've seen her put on makeup and do her hair only to sit on the couch and binge watch whatever TV show has her interest at the moment. "You look great by the way."

"Thanks." Her cheeks turn a soft shade of pink.

I wonder how long I've had this effect on her, and how I've never noticed. To be fair, she's always been great at hiding her emotions. It's one of the things she's excelled at since she's the youngest of six. Even though she almost always got her way, she never wanted to do anything to tip the boat.

"I'm going to wait in the living room." I point my thumb over my shoulder. Crowding her is the last thing I want to do, and that's what this feels like. She has a process when she's getting ready to go somewhere. Just because we're officially dating doesn't mean I should be encroaching on that.

"That's cool. I'll be ready in ten. I just need to find my shoes."

A small chuckle comes out of me as I turn toward the door. The office at Starlit Fields is incredibly organized. Not a paperclip out of place. But her closet...that's an entirely different story.

It's like there are two versions of her. One that allows herself to be carefree in her own space, and the other completely aware of where everything is. Everything in my professional life and home is slightly messy. It's clean, but cluttered. Bad habits I picked up from my parents and I've been working to fix for years.

While she finishes getting ready, I head to the kitchen. For some reason nerves are setting in. This is the first time we've been out and about in Asheville since we became official. I kind of understand why she's getting ready, and going all out. It's almost like an armor for her.

When we were in high school, she'd come to school with a full face of makeup and her hair curled. It was how she showed up to take tests or do anything she was afraid of. I guess it made her powerful and like she could accomplish anything.

I wonder if it was something she picked up in the intro to theatre class we took. It was a blow off class for me. Anytime we did shows, I would work on the tech side. But she loved stepping into a new character. She could be anyone she wanted without any fears.

I wonder how her life would have turned out if she'd stay in theatre classes. If she would have left Asheville for good. Or, if she would have stayed to fulfill the obligation she feels toward her family business. I guess we'll never know.

I grab a bottle of wine and a glass. A little liquid courage never hurt anyone. The need to force my nerves to settle down is not something I anticipated. I take a sip and let the sangria work its magic through my nervous system.

"Oh, I didn't realize we were starting the night early."

The wine sloshes in the glass as I jump. A quick check confirms none of it spilled on me.

"Do you want a glass?" I point toward the cabinet.

"Nope, I'm starving. Are you ready?" Her eyes bounce toward the glass in my hand then back to me. A sign to finish up before she gets hangry.

Tilting the glass up, I drink the last bit of wine. "Yep." I quickly wash and dry the glass before setting it back in its spot on the counter. The cork goes back into the bottle. I'm sure we'll finish that off as soon as we get back from dinner.

"Ready to face the fine citizens of Asheville?"

She scoffs. "Please most of the people are probably running their kids around and getting ready for a weekend of little league games."

She's not wrong.

I place my hand on the small of her back, and she leans into me. Being able to touch her freely without second guessing is the confidence boost I need.

Who knew I would be this shaken up having her by my side like this after being a part of her life for over a decade.

nineteen

· · ·

piper

ONE THING I am not prepared for as we make our public debut is the stares we are getting from everyone. People get together and break up in this town all the damn time. Why are we the center of everyone's attention? Everyone we pass from the car to the restaurant glances at our hands and then has a weird smile on their face. It's not like we've never held hands in public before.

Beau squeezes my hand as he opens the door to our favorite Mexican restaurant. The quiet encouragement manages to soothe my annoyance with people.

In just a few steps we're standing at the counter. The person standing there looks at us then shuffles through some things in front of the register. His eyes are wide as he glances between me and Beau. "We don't have a to-go order for you. Did you call one in?"

The fact they know us this well is kind of sad. We always grab food and go home. Both of us have to deal with people on a daily basis and it's our one time to decompress.

"Um, no." Beau blushes and it's adorable. "We'd actually like to eat here tonight."

The employee's eyes widen at our unexpected request. We've managed to throw him off his game. "Let me see if we have any tables available."

"Thanks," I add softly before he rushes off. "By his reaction, you'd think we blew his mind."

Beau laughs and pulls me closer to him. "Can you blame him? It's been years since we've actually eaten inside. He might think we're doppelgängers or something."

"Please, if we were some sort of supernatural being, would we be so stressed all the time?"

His only answer is a shrug. It's likely we'd still be maxed out to capacity, but I think the stressors would be slightly different. Like trying to stay in one place without folks noticing we don't age.

"We have a table for you." Whoa, he popped up out of nowhere. "Follow me."

Whispers surround us as we wind our way through the tables to the single table without a patron. And it's right in the middle of the room. Great, now we really won't be able to hide from the masses. Not that I'm worried what they think about me and Beau being a couple, but because it's none of their damn business.

This also explains why we had to park in front of Whoopsie Daisy. This place is packed. So much for parents running their kids around.

Once we're seated, we're handed menus. I take my

time looking over it while pretending not to hear the people at the table next to us.

"I told you there were a thing. I heard they were making out in front of everyone at the carnival last weekend."

"I always knew something was going on between them. A guy and a girl can never be just friends. And the way they've been inseparable since we were kids is weird."

My knuckles are turning white from the grip I have on the menu. What right do these women have to question anything between me and Beau. They were assholes in high school and it appears that hasn't changed…at all.

I turn my head to tell them they are doing a shitty job of whispering, but a hand on mine stops me. The soft caress brings me back to my own space and calms the rage building inside of me.

He mouths, "It's not worth it." He's right. I know that. But just once I wish someone would stand up to these mean girls and put them in their place.

Our waitress shows up with a beaming smile and places a basket of chips and a bowl of salsa between us. At least someone is happy to see us. "What can I get you to drink? Soda, margaritas…wine?" She winks at me. It's funny because I know they carry our wine, but that's just not strong enough for tonight.

"Margarita, please. Strong."

The smirk Beau gives me is annoying. He knows the reason I need it is so I don't go off on our former classmates.

"I'll have a margarita, too. Normal, please."

"Smart ass," I mutter under my breath.

The waitress laughs and turns toward the bar. "I'll be back with your drinks and to take your order."

"Thanks." I call out to her. "Is it wrong that I hope they leave sooner rather than later." My voice is barely a whisper because I know how to do it correctly and not be heard by neighboring tables.

Beau leans forward and grabs a chip before dipping it into the salsa. "If they are still anything like they were in high school, I think we're shit out of luck. They'll stay as long as they can so they have something to gossip about tomorrow."

Ugh, he's probably right. They were always the last to leave parties and the first to say some horrible shit about people at school when we went back. Honestly, I don't know why they kept getting invited. I would have flipped them the finger and moved on.

I need to change the subject before I lose my shit. "So, how was work today?"

He scrubs a hand over his face. "It was fine. The boss called me in his office to ask how the marketing we're doing is going."

"That's good, isn't it?" He's finally being recognized for the amazing work he does.

"Yes?"

"You don't sound too sure about that."

Our drinks are here and we give the waitress our order before turning back to the conversation.

"No, it's good. But…he keeps talking about me moving up the ranks and I'm not sure I want to do that. And Cole keeps trying to buddy up to me because I'm getting his uncle's attention."

"Oh, that's gross." I take a sip of my margarita, and it's

exactly what I wanted. "He's the one that keeps trying to give his shit to you to do, right?"

"Yep. He's kind of a douchebag, and everyone knows it. But, they're scared to say anything because they don't want to get fired."

"Double gross." My nose scrunches in disgust. "Getting a promotion wouldn't be a bad thing."

"Except I'd have to work with the bigger companies, and I don't want to do that. I love focusing on the little guy. Helping a small business find their footing and grow into something amazing is where my passion lies. I think it's because I spent so much time at the winery with you. Seeing how every day, normal people succeed is what it's all about for me."

"Glad I could be an inspiration." The small bow I add in has him rolling his eyes. "So, what are you going to do? You realize you could probably branch out on your own. You would do amazing things for the small businesses here."

"The thought has been bouncing around in here." He taps his forehead. "But…it would be a drastic pay cut until I get a big enough customer base."

Therein always lies the problem with trying to start a new business on your own. It's rocky until you can find your customer base. It makes me wonder how my family did it when they opened the winery all those years ago. There wasn't an easy way to get the word out. At least, not like there is now.

"It's doable though, right?" The last thing I want is for him to be miserable in his job. And honestly, after my dad sees the numbers, we've been doing, he'd probably pay

Beau for all his hard work helping me get the social media campaigns off the ground.

"Of course, but I don't want to eat through my savings just yet." He eats another chip and shrugs his shoulders. "For now, I'll wait and see what the boss offers me after he sees the success. Maybe I'll have done so well, he'll let me decide what I want to do. Because being in management for anyone but myself does not sound appealing to me."

I get that. It's even part of the pain point with the winery. Even though there's no true boss vs employee hierarchy since Dad wants us to run it equally, it does suck having to check in with Pierce all the time. In his eyes, and Dad's, he gets a bit of seniority because he's the oldest. If Paula was still officially part of the winery, I wonder how the dynamic would work. I'm sure it would be slightly different.

"Well, I support you no matter what you decide to do." I slide my foot forward gently rubbing it against his as a sign of affirmation. Putting my hand on his would have probably been better, but I have a chip in one and my margarita in the other. Quite frankly, I'm not setting either of those down.

"Ar—are you playing footsies with me?" The false shock on his face is adorable. "You better stop before the jerks next to us take notice."

"Like I care what they think." I set down my drink and flip my hair over my shoulder. "Let them talk. It's all they know how to do."

A loud slam comes from the table next to us. Out of the corner of my eye I watch as they scoot their chairs out and stomp toward the door. Serves them right for listening in.

"They looked like someone just pissed in their cereal." Beau laughs.

Shrugging, I pick up my drink just as the waitress brings us our food. "They needed to hear it. Nobody likes a gossip."

Beau thanks the waitress for our order and digs in. "Says the girl who knows pretty much everything going on with her siblings."

"That's expected." I build my fajita taco. "Siblings know each other's dirt. It's like a law or something."

He laughs as he takes another bite and almost chokes.

"See what happens when you're a smart ass. Next thing you know you'll be slamming down the check and marching out of the restaurant in a fit."

He takes a drink to get his coughing under control. "Don't say funny shit when I'm eating and I won't almost die."

"Dramatics don't look good on you, Beau." I take a bite of my food and it's even better when it's fresh from the kitchen. Don't get me wrong, I love eating in the comfort of my home when we get takeout, but this is so good. We also never run out of salsa.

His margarita is gone and he's switched to water. It's a good thing, too. When I said to make it strong, they did. There's no way in hell I'm driving anywhere.

"So, what do you want to do when we leave here? The night is still young." He waggles his eyebrows up and down.

"We're in Asheville, there isn't much to do. We can get ice cream, go to the park, or go home and watch a movie." I take another bite and swallow before adding, "Those are the picks. Not much to do in a town this size, and I don't really feel like going to Out of the Ashes."

"Me either," he agrees. "We'll figure it out."

This is one of the things I love about him. He asks for my input and doesn't assume I want to do something. If I don't know…he's okay with that. It's the way we've always operated.

He was right of course. Nothing changed in our friendship when we admitted we had feelings for each other. If anything, it's brought us closer. There's a deeper level of comfort we haven't felt before. Like we can finally be ourselves around each other. It's refreshing in a way I never thought possible. No wonder nothing ever worked out with guys I've dated. They aren't him.

"Why are you staring at me like that?" Beau grabs his napkin from his lap and rubs it over his chin. "Do I have something on my face?"

"I'm only admiring the view."

"That was cheesy as hell, even for you." He shakes his head and keeps eating. I swear he doesn't take the time to appreciate his food. He inhales it like he's never eaten a day in his life.

I on the other hand like to take my time. He gives me crap for being a slow eater, but I don't care.

"Yeah, yeah." I wave away his comment and glance down at my plate of food. I've barely made a dent in half of it. "I think I'm going to need a box."

"I'll get one. Hang tight." He leaves the table in search of our waitress.

I can't help watching him walk away. The way his jeans hug his butt in just the right way. The way he's attentive to what I want or need. What's not to love about him? Being able to show my feelings in the open is freeing in a way I never thought it could be.

twenty

. . .

beau

IT'S way too damn hot to be outside doing this. Why Piper felt the need to do the outside filming today, I'll have no idea. Actually, I do know. It's the only way we'll avoid Pierce. Because she doesn't know that he knows what we're doing. Keeping this secret from her is eating at me.

"No, not like that." Piper swipes at my hand and wine sloshes over the side. Please don't be on my white shirt. I didn't bring anything to change into. A quick glance down shows no red stains. Thank God.

"What do you mean not like this?" I lift the glass in question. "There's only so many ways to hold a glass of wine."

All she does is laugh. I don't see what's so funny. It's not like I'm a huge wine drinker. Half the time when we're at my house, we drink out of mason jars. They were cheap when I bought my house and needed glasses. I'm pretty sure she has some of them at her house.

"Just be a little gentler with the glass. You don't have to hold onto it for dear life." She lifts a second glass. Her fingers on either side of the stem. It's delicate. "I'm not saying it has to be a dainty hold, but at least don't look like you're about to snap it in half. It ruins the vibe I'm going for."

"Which is what?" I glance around me to see if anyone is coming. I don't want her brother to catch us because he'll act like he didn't know anything about it. "I'm not sure I'm the right person to capture the vibe."

"Believe me." Her eyes trail over me from head to toe. "You're perfect for it. Or, do you not remember all the comments we got from the stories I shared that one night? Most of those questions wanted to know about you."

I lean across the table toward her. "And you're okay with sharing me with the masses?"

Piper's back straightens and I swear she lets out a tiny growl. Possessiveness is the last thing I expected from her. She's so free-spirited and goes with the flow. I guess it's different when we're dating. Though, maybe now she knows how I felt watching her go on all those dates over the years.

"They will know you aren't available."

"What are you going to do make a t-shirt that says 'Piper's Property'?"

"If I have to." She takes a sip of her wine. "Now, let's try this again. We're a couple on a romantic date at the winery."

From my point of view, that's exactly what we are. We don't have to pretend. "How are you going to record the video if you're in it? I know there are timers, but I don't know that you can run that fast and not look out of breath."

"I'm magic." She holds up a small device. "Now, lean close like we were before and act like we are having a conversation. Don't worry about them hearing what you're saying. I'll take that out when I edit it."

"Okay. Let's do this." I wait for her to press a button on the remote and hold my glass between us as I lean forward. "So how was your day?"

She's fighting the urge to roll her eyes. Annoyed isn't the look she's going for. Instead, she smiles as if I've said the most endearing thing in the world. "You should know. I've been with you most of it."

I take a small sip. Guzzling the glass of wine probably doesn't fit the look she's going for. "Believe me. I know. If I could wake up to you in one of my shirts every morning, I would be in heaven."

She starts to laugh, but gets herself under control. "We might be able to arrange that."

"And cut." A voice from the direction of the phone startles me. Parker is beaming at the two of us. Paula is walking up behind him. "I think that was a great shot."

"What are y'all doing here?" I'm confused. Piper has all but sworn me to secrecy, but two of her siblings are here.

"I need them for a couple of videos. I know I can get some stock videos off a website, but I figured it would be much better if we have footage of the actual winery. Besides, I've already made Parker pour wine into a glass for me."

"I haven't seen that video yet."

"Because I haven't posted it." Now she freely rolls her

eyes at me. "I want to get some video of me and Paula relaxing with a glass of wine. Then the four of us hanging out like friends."

"Pfft. We are friend's little sister." Parker grins and motions for him to join me behind the camera. "But we better move fast. Pierce said he was coming to check inventory at some point today."

"You know I hate when you call me that. I have a name." Piper waves her sister over. "Let me refill the glasses really quick."

"I didn't know we were also drinking the wine." Paula glances around, nervous someone is going to catch us.

"Well, I'm sure as hell not going to let it go to waste." She studies her sister. "Just pretend like you're drinking it. But later…you're telling me why you aren't drinking."

Paula has never been a big drinker. I don't know why Piper is surprised she isn't drinking. Even when we were in high school, she always offered to be our driver. How many older siblings would do that? Especially when they aren't even in school anymore.

They sit there and whisper about something, look toward us, then bust out laughing. What the hell are they talking about?

"Are we going to do this thing? Or, play with fate and have to explain what we're doing?" Parker asks.

"Okay, okay." Piper grunts. She clicks the button and the two of them laugh like they are having the time of their lives. Theatre classes really paid off for Piper. But I didn't know Paula could act so carefree at the drop of a hate.

"Hey, how is it recording? I didn't press anything." Parker points at the phone.

"Your little sister is pure magic."

"Ugh, please tell me you actually mean that, and it's not code for some sexual thing between you."

I lean over laughing and almost knock the phone over. To Piper and Paula's credit, they act like I'm not being a massive disruption.

Once I have my amusement in check, I shake my head at Parker. "She has a remote. And I would never talk to you about stuff with your sister. At least, not in that aspect. There are boundaries you just don't cross."

"Good answer." He glances at the phone. "Well, she pressed the stop button. I guess it's time for us to join the scene."

We each grab a chair and join them at the table. It's small, and the four of us barely fit, but it's enough to get a good video…hopefully.

"What was so funny?" Piper lifts an eyebrow in question. She's always been able to do that, and would laugh anytime I tried. She said it looks like I'm blinking extra hard when I try.

"Start the video." I bump into her shoulder. "It'll be a good laugh to catch amongst friends."

It's a good thing Parker is sitting opposite of me. He looks like he wants to punch me in the shoulder.

Piper presses play and I wait a few seconds before telling them about the exchange. Parker has a scowl the whole time.

As soon as I get to the comment he made, both Piper and Paula start laughing. Parker moves his shoulders up and down to imitate the action but he doesn't find it amusing at all. He's usually the one who doesn't take anything seriously.

After Piper stops the recording, she studies her brother. "Why are you so mad? It was funny."

"I don't know how I feel about being the butt of the joke."

"That figures," Paula mumbles. The only reason I can hear her is because I'm sitting right next to her. "You can dish it out, but you can't take it."

"You know how I am about my ego." He holds a hand to his chest. "It can only take so much emotional turmoil."

"You're so full of shit." I laugh. "Who's up for going to Out of the Ashes? I'm craving wings."

"I'm down," Parker says.

"I can't go." Paula shakes her head. "Tristan is about to be in the studio with Crooked Halo, and who knows when we'll be able to have another date night."

"Go spend time with your man." Piper shoos away her sister. "But remind him not to let work consume him. It's no way to live."

"Says the baby sibling who always gets her way."

"Not always." Piper tilts her head to the side. "I mean, I'm kind of being a rebel right now because Pierce said no. All of this is behind his back."

"True, but you're still doing it anyway." Paula bends down to give her sister a hug. "Just know when Pierce finds out, because he will, I'll have your back."

I don't miss the pointed look she shoots at their brother. If I had to guess it's a subtle threat that he better have it too.

"Have fun tonight." I wave at Paula as she walks toward the front of the building. "Don't do anything we wouldn't do."

"Or do!" Piper adds.

"I'm going to need both of you to be less gross if we're going to the bar." He waves his hands between us. "Don't get me wrong, I'm glad y'all have figured your shit out, but all the emotions is just too much for me."

"You're so full of shit." Piper stands and grabs the glasses off the table. Most of them are empty aside from Paula's. Piper chugs it. "Beau, can you hand me that box? And Parker, take these chairs back to the other table."

"Sure, you ask him all sweetly, but you order me. I see how it is."

"Yeah, that's because I get to see him na—"

"For the love of God do not finish that sentence."

I hand him my chair as I get up before grabbing the box for Piper. She sets the empty glasses in it, and adds the empty bottle next. "Do you need me to get anything else?"

"Nope, that's all I need to take back to my house. We'll need to stop there before we head to Ashes."

"Why?" She looks fine in what she's wearing. It's not like they have a dress code. Not yet, anyway. If they keep on the trajectory of being the bar to hang out in, that may change.

"To drop these off." She points at the box then moves to the tripod holding her phone. "I know you're a good driver and all, but on the off chance we get pulled over for anything…"

She lets the sentence drop off because I know exactly what she means. The last thing we want to do is have to explain why we have an empty wine bottle and glasses. Most of the cops in this town know the Summers, but I don't think they'd let us slip by with that.

"I hope it's cool I invited your brother." I didn't even

think to ask before I did. Maybe she wanted the two of us to be alone tonight. Either way I'm happy.

"Please, I have plans when we get there."

"What do you mean?"

"He shouldn't have let us know that us doing couple things would bug him. I plan on torturing him."

Shaking my head I turn toward the front and head to my car. I'll never understand the need for siblings to get under each other's skin.

That doesn't mean I'm not going to enjoy watching Parker squirm. Like he's always said, we're like family and I might also be okay with pestering him the way a sibling would. Tonight is going to be a blast.

twenty-one

. . .

piper

BEING MORE than best friends with Beau the past few weeks has been amazing. Instead of causing friction, it's only brought us closer together. I don't have to pretend I'm something I'm not with him. He knows me inside and out. From the awkward teenage years when I wore bad clothing styles to learning my way around the local college. He's seen me find myself along the way.

Having him by my side as a boyfriend…is the cherry on top. He knows what I need before I do, and he's helping me find who I am in a relationship. A small part of me finds it odd that he's even by my side for this. There really was a reason none of the dates I went on didn't work out. I've spent the whole time comparing them to him.

My phone dings with a text message. Beau isn't supposed to be here for another hour to go to the water-park. One of the perks of school being back in session is we can enjoy the park without dodging a bunch of kids. Well, at least until they close for the season.

I set down my sunscreen and check my phone. My eyes widen at the name, and I don't know if I should even open it. It feels unfair not to, though. Ugh, I did not sign up for these grown people problems.

Reluctantly, I open the message to see what it says.

ROB

I know it's been a minute, but I wanted to give you some space. I was wondering if you'd like to go on that second date.

The one date I went on where there was a chance of another one. If there was one person that could hold a candle to the man Beau is, it's Rob.

Regret works its way through my body. Not because I wish I was with Rob. Never that. But because I gave him my number. I've never done that with someone I've met off the dating app. It's easier to avoid them if they message me in app.

Who knows, maybe Rob did message me on the app. I wouldn't know because I deleted them the day after the funhouse. It was the only way I could ensure I gave me and Beau a fair shot without having the ability to run scared. I know myself well enough to know it was a possibility. He probably did, too.

How do I let him down easy? I don't want to come off as a bitch, or mean. I swipe away from the message and call my sister.

"Hello?" She picks up after the first ring.

"How do you break things off with someone without being mean?"

There's silence on the other end. "You're already breaking up with Beau?"

"No." I'm offended she can even think that. "The guy I went on a date with before me and Beau became a thing just texted me asking me about a second date."

She sighs, as if I'm taking up too much of her time. "You called me at work for…this."

"To be fair, I've never been in this position before. Most of my dates I walked out of before they were over."

"Okay." I can imagine her pinching the bridge of her nose in frustration. I get it. I'd probably be the same way, too. "Either don't text him back. It's probably the safest route. Or, because I know you won't do that, let him know you're seeing someone and you wish him the best. If he texts you back after that, block him."

"You make it sound so simple."

"Because it is. You're the one making it complicated." I can hear the shop doorbell in the background. "I've got a customer. You can do this."

She hangs up before I can even say bye. She knows that's one of my pet peeves.

Taking a deep breath, I open up the text because my sister is right, I can't ignore it. That feels cruel. I can do this, though.

PIPER

> I hope you're doing well. I'm sorry, I can't. I've started seeing someone.

I hit send before I second guess myself. His response comes immediately. Was he waiting by his phone? I hope not.

ROB

That's cool. I wish you the best.

Maybe Paula was right. His reply doesn't sound as if he's mad. Maybe a bit passive aggressive. But he could have been cruel since I didn't let him know immediately after the date.

Not my problem anymore. I delete his number and toss my phone on my bed. Digging through my bag, I see what all I've packed. I still need a towel and some clothes to change into. There's no way in hell I'm riding home damp. It's never a fun experience.

Hurrying to the bathroom, I grab a towel before searching for extra clothes. I don't need anything fancy, but maybe more than leggings and a t-shirt in case Beau wants to stop for dinner on the way back.

I shove all the items into my bag and move to the living room. He can't blame me not being ready today. It wouldn't matter though because today I get to spend the day with my boyfriend. The term fills me with so much excitement it's ridiculous.

"Let's go in the lazy river." I motion Beau to follow me. "It's practically empty."

There are still quite a few people here, but it looks like it's those with littles or wanting to avoid teenagers. Apparently, we all had the same idea today.

"Do you realize how much pee is probably in that?" He shakes his head and crosses his arms over his chest. Defiant

Beau is a sexy Beau. I've always thought this, but now I can ogle him freely. "Don't think you undressing me with your eyes is going to make me budge. It's not happening."

"That's usually kids, and there aren't many here outside of those in the area specifically for children."

"It's funny you think adults don't do it, too." He takes a few steps toward me and pulls me into his arms.

It's hot and he's sweaty, but I don't mind. I'll let him hold me no matter what. For the longest time I only let him hold me after a bad date or a fight with my siblings. This is different. He's holding me because he wants to. Because he wants me. And the thought of him letting me go one day sends a pang of panic throughout my body.

Shaking that I away, I look up at him with my biggest puppy dog eyes. He's never been able to resist them. "Please? Besides don't most places like this have that chemical in the water that shows when people pee." I glance toward the river and the crystal blue water. "I don't see any color puddles anywhere."

He kisses the top of my head and squeezes me in a bear hug. "You better be happy I love you. I wouldn't go traipsing into a germ ridden river for anyone."

Love falling from his lips has my knees buckling. We've said it a million times before, but never since we've started seeing each other romantically. I'm not sure which way I should take it. I'm choosing not to overthink it and roll with it.

"How many lakes and creeks have we swam in?" I pull away to lead him toward the river, grabbing a tube on the way. "I'm pretty sure those have more germs than this."

"Probably." He shrugs as he helps me into the circle tube. "The only difference is those are out in nature. I fully expect to swim with fish and there to be germs. This place is man made. There's a difference."

"If you say so." There's no point in arguing with him. I got him to come in with me to wind down, and that's all that matters. The only thing that would make this better is a margarita in my hand.

He climbs into his own tube, and reaches for my hand to tether us together. "Are you good?"

"Yep." I close my eyes and lean my head back. "This is the life. We should play hooky more often. Floating here is way better than working."

"Sadly, we can't live on river vibes." He pulls my float closer to his with so much force I almost fall off.

My eyes jerk open and I see there is someone ahead of us and I would have ran right into them. "Thanks for the save."

"Forever."

Commitment has always terrified me. But him saying that one word doesn't make me want to run for the hills. I was always so worried about choosing the wrong person to spend my life with, but with Beau…it wouldn't be the wrong person. Not that he wouldn't always be in my life as a friend or anything. It's just much nicer with him as a partner. Someone to take on the world with. Which is why I need to tell him about the text I received this morning.

"So, I got a text this morning." Yes, it's a dumb way to open up the conversation. It's hard though. We're solid, I know that. He's always been more understanding than anyone else I know. But this is different because now we are so much more.

"Oh yeah? Was it Hollywood trying to draw you away after the videos we made over the weekend?" He laughs because he knows damn well, I haven't posted them yet. He has alerts set for my posts so he can see how they are doing. Honestly, at this point, I should probably give him access to our accounts.

"Pfft." I wave away his ridiculous comment. "Do you think I'd be here if they did?"

"Yes. As much as you complain about your siblings, I don't think you could leave them." He gives my hand a squeeze. "So, who was this mystery message from?"

There's no way to gently say it. "Rob."

The grip he has on my hand loosens the slightest bit. Like I could pull my hand away if I wanted to…I don't.

"Wh-what did he say?" Beau has never sounded unsure of himself in his life. Right now, he sounds like he's seconds away from questioning all his life decisions.

"He asked if I was interested in that second date." There's no use in letting him think I even considered it. "I told him I was seeing someone, and he wished us the best."

His sigh of relief is loud enough to be heard over the water lapping against the sides of our floats. He was actually worried I would go on that second date. Maybe he doesn't have as much trust in me as I do in him.

We pass by a small group of women who just entered the river. It's probably one of my favorite parts about this certain attraction. We aren't stuck going all the way around. We can get on or off wherever we want. I used to get out sooner than my siblings because they terrorized me when we came in.

"Thanks for letting me know." His voice is thick and pulls me away from memory lane. "I know you didn't have to. We never said whether or not we were exclusive."

"As if I could date anyone else while dating you." He knows damn well, I'm pretty exclusive when I'm dating someone. Not that there's been many people who've made it past a couple of months. I'm not the sort of person to play the field.

"Oh, I know that. I just wonder if me declaring my feelings may have messed up something with him. You talked about a second date, and you never do that unless you're interested."

Okay, I can't take any more of this gloomy shit. He needs to know exactly where I stand. Right here and right now.

I slide off my float and almost go under because it's so abrupt. Luckily, the water isn't deep and I gain my footing quickly. I pull him to the side where most moms have their toddlers. I don't want to be in the way.

Looping my arm through my float, I place both hands on the side of his float. No doubt I look ridiculous trying to avoid getting hit in the face with mine. But he needs to see me for this.

"You. Do. Not. Have. Anything. To. Worry. About." Hopefully he gets the point. "I've had a crush on you for years, but I didn't want to rock the boat. There's no chance in hell I was going to throw this away for a second date with someone who doesn't hold a candle to you."

He stares at me. It's the first time I've ever been this direct with him when it comes to my feelings. I usually brush things to the side, unless it has to do with my brothers. He gets to hear all those passion filled rants. It's not easy for me to shock him, and I'd be lying if I said it wasn't satisfying.

Beau holds his hands up in surrender. "You don't have

to talk to me like I'm five. I know you would never do that to me."

"Apparently, I do." I shove my float next to his and almost hit a passerby. "Now, stop moping and help me get back into my float. We're not done enjoying the day."

There's no argument from him. He hooks his foot around the pole by the entrance and holds my float with one hand while using the other to give me balance as I climb my way back in.

Hopefully this cures any and all doubts he might have about us. "Oh yeah, I forgot to tell you. Mom and Dad are having a cookout next weekend and told me to invite you."

"Have I ever not been invited?"

"No, but I guess since we're dating, they want it to be a little more formal." At least my family loves Beau. They always have.

twenty-two

. . .

beau

PIPER'S ADMISSION has been eating at me since we left the waterpark. She truly didn't have to because I completely trust her. More than she should be trusting me considering the secret I'm harboring.

In over ten years of being friends, we've never lied to each other. While I haven't flat out lied, I'm omitting the role her brother is playing in our marketing efforts. It's practically the same thing.

My phone rings. Mr. Gardner's name flashing across the screen. It's Saturday, what the hell does he want? Fear that something happened with one of my accounts courses through my body. That's the only reason he would be calling me on the weekend.

"Hello?" I can't keep the confusion from seeping through the greeting.

"Hi, Beau. Sorry to bug you on the weekend," Mr.

Gardner says as if he really is apologetic about interrupting my weekend.

Hopefully this call doesn't take long. I'm supposed to head up to the winery soon.

"It's okay. Is everything okay? Is there an issue with one of my clients?"

"Oh no, nothing as serious as that." I can picture him waving my concern away with his hands. If his hands aren't crossed in front of him, or shoved into his pockets, he's very much a hand talker.

"What can I help you with?"

"It's more like how I can help you." He pauses for a moment to see if I'm going to take the bait. I'm not. "I've been looking over the numbers you've sent me on this passion project, and I'm impressed."

"Thank you, sir." I'm not sure what else he wants me to say.

"You're welcome. I want to offer you a promotion."

"That's incredible."

"I know you mentioned wanting to work exclusively with small businesses, but we don't have a ton of those coming through the firm. The few we do have, you're already working with. You would lead up the team on mid-size businesses. They have more money to play with so you could scale up what you've already been doing. You'd have your own office and of course a raise. What do you say?"

This really could have waited until Monday, but I can't tell him that. "That's a great offer. Can I think about it over the weekend?"

"Sure, sure." I just know he's leaning back in his chair,

hands steepled over his stomach. "But don't wait too long."

"I won't. Thank you for the opportunity, Mr. Gardner."

"Have a great rest of the weekend."

Talk about a call I wasn't expecting. It's a great offer, but I wouldn't be working with the businesses I want. And, even though he didn't say it, I know I'll be working longer hours. The guys who work with those, and bigger, companies are workaholics with no life.

Evenings and weekends are something I treasure, especially with Piper. Before I make any decisions, I want to get her perspective. Her opinion is the only thing that matters to me.

With my phone still in hand, I call her.

"Hey." She answers on the first ring, and I can hear some kind of noise in the background. It sounds like she's outside. Maybe she's watering her flower garden. She's turned into quite the green thumb over the past couple of years.

"Hi. Do I need to scoop you up on my way to the winery?" By being her ride, I've always been her excuse to leave family functions when her brothers get to be too much.

"I wish," she sighs. "Peter pulled up to my house about thirty minutes ago in a golf cart. Apparently, my help is needed with setting up tables."

"That sounds fun," I laugh.

"I honestly don't see why I need to help. There are six of us. Surely, the rest of them are more than capable of doing it without bothering me."

"You are a Summers, you have to help. Mom's rule," Peter says loud enough I can hear him.

"We literally only need three tables put up. It takes less than two minutes."

"Argue with Mom, then. I'm only doing what I'm told."

This is a common occurrence when I'm on the phone with Piper. Even when we were teenagers, there was always a chance she'd be having two conversations while on the phone with me.

"Because that's all you know how to do," she mumbles. It's low enough only I hear it. If Peter heard it, he'd be throwing a tantrum.

"Should I head that way and save you? Sounds like your siblings are already picking on you."

"Only if you want to." She sighs and I can imagine her running her hand through her hair, doing everything she can to keep her cool and not cause any waves. "Just let me know when you get here and I'll meet you up front."

"Are we doing the cookout at the winery or your parents' house?"

"Mom and Dad's. They don't want us making the grassy areas by the tables a mess."

"I'll see you in a few. Try not to murder your brother before I get there."

"I can't make any promises," she sing-songs. "See you in a bit. Bye."

"Bye."

When I get there, I'll pull her away to tell her about the promotion, and finally unburden myself from this secret. It's only fair to be completely honest with her, just like she has been with me.

"Can you grab that dish and bring it out to the patio?" Mrs. Summers asks as she backs toward the door with some sort of dessert in her hands.

"Sure thing." I pick up the dish in question and follow her outside. I think it's potato salad. It doesn't look like the one she normally makes, and I wonder if she's experimenting in the kitchen again.

After setting the dish on the table holding all the food, I search for Piper. As soon as I pulled in her mom put me to work. I didn't even get to tell Piper hello. Now I get where Peter is coming from. I mean, Mrs. Summers has always treated me like one of her own, but she's never made me do anything.

Not that she forced me to help, I could have said no. How could I, though? I spent most of my teenage years in this very yard. Even in my college years after I went no contact with my parents because they were horrible and didn't give a shit about me. The Summers were always there to make me feel like I belonged.

"There you are!" Piper jumps into my arms, hers going around my neck. I almost fall backward with the force, but catch myself on a nearby tree. "I didn't think Mom was ever going to release you from her clutches."

I shrug my shoulder. "You know I'm always willing to help."

"Maybe a little too much." She gives me a quick peck on the cheek. "You don't have to prove your worthiness to them. You'll always have a place here."

"I know." I sigh. "I just feel like I owe it to your parents for pretty much taking me in this whole time."

"You owe them nothing. Believe me, they are happy to have you around. Sometimes I think you might be their favorite." She says the last sentence in a whisper as if afraid someone will overhear.

"Please." I shake my head. "You are the baby, you'll always be the favorite."

"Maybe." She tilts her head to the side. "But that doesn't really matter as long as I'm your favorite."

Her lips crash into mine and I lean against the tree, letting her fall further into me. Being with Piper feels like home. Like this is right where I'm supposed to be. Wrapped up in her without a care in the world.

When she pulls away, I fight the urge to reel her back into me. "I need to tell you something."

"Uh oh." She cocks her head. "That doesn't sound good."

"My boss called and offered me a promotion based on our efforts with Starlit Fields."

"That's amazing."

"Yeah, it is." I'll tell her the part about her brother knowing later…when we're alone. Then she can lash out at me in private and I won't subject her family to me getting my ass chewed out.

"Why don't you sound happy about it?" The concern she shows makes me feel like a bigger ass for not being honest.

"I won't be helping small businesses anymore. He plans to move me over the bigger businesses. Which is great because there's a chance for a higher commission, but I don't want to work the hours."

"Doesn't everyone have the same hours as you?"

"Yeah, but they are always at the beck and call of their clients. Most of them end up working evenings and weekends. That isn't something I want to do...especially now."

"Yeah, that sounds gross. I don't even work every weekend here." She looks over her shoulder. "The one perk of working with family is they enforce rotation on the weekend shifts, so we pretty much only work one weekend a month. Unless you're Pierce. He doesn't know how to do anything but work here."

"See, that's the type of person I'm trying not to become. I don't want to work to live." I glance down at her. "What do you think I should do?"

"How long do you have to mull it over?"

"At least the weekend." I glance at the leaves above us. They almost form a bubble between us and the rest of the world. "But he told me not to take too long because he might offer it to someone else."

"Everyone, get up here. It's time to eat!" Mrs. Summers's voice carries from the patio. That woman has a set of lungs on her. It was probably necessary when trying to get all the kids in one area.

Piper shakes her head. "My sister must have finally made it. We can talk it over more tomorrow, or when we get home tonight. We'll figure out which course of action you should take."

I like how she says we. Like I'm not in this alone. Which I know, of course. She's always been the one I've talked to when I need to make a decision. Only this time, we'll be making the decision for us. Or, at least, I hope so.

She grabs my hand and pulls me along behind toward the patio. All the Summers kids are gathered around tables. We're lucky enough to get to the table with Paula and Parker. I guess Tristan is in the studio and couldn't make it.

Peter and Philip are talking at a table on the opposite side of the patio, leaving the one in the middle empty. Pierce is standing next to his parents. Why does it feel like they are about to say something important? I thought this was only a small cookout.

"Can I have everyone's attention?" Mr. Summers's voice booms over the quiet conversations. He waits until we're all silent before continuing. "As you know I've been planning on retiring for quite some time. Well, your mom wants to go on a cruise, and I figured what better time than now."

"What?" Piper's voice is a whisper of disbelief. "You implied it would be years." Her voice is loud enough to be heard over whatever else her dad is saying.

"Not now, Piper." Pierce admonishes her as if she's a child.

"Oh, you feel all big and bad because you're the one in charge now." She glances around at her siblings. "Did the rest of you know this was happening?"

Parker has the good sense to look away. Philip, Peter, and Paula look as if they are just as surprised as Piper.

"Sweetheart," her dad says in the soothing tone he always used when she got hurt. "Pierce is not in charge. You all are going to work together, and if you don't then I'll sell the winery."

That's not a step I ever thought I'd see him take. Paula doesn't have anything to lose or gain in this fight because she walked away from the family business years ago. She just now started connecting the winery with events, but none of those have happened yet.

Tears well up in Piper's eyes. "You can't sell the winery. It's our family legacy."

"Which is why I hope the five of you can work together." He takes a look at his wife and smiles at her. They deserve the chance to travel the world and enjoy some time away from the winery. "We've put in a lot of years here and set y'all up for success. You've all been running the winery yourselves for the past few years. Keep doing that, and you won't even notice I'm not a part of the daily grind."

Piper nods, not trusting her voice to say anything else. I know she's thinking of all the ways things may fail, but they've got this. She's got this.

"Alright everyone, let's eat." Mrs. Summers takes a step back to let everyone form a line.

With everyone busy, Piper takes that moment to stand. "I need a minute." Then she's rushing off the patio and around the house.

I get up to follow her, but Paula lays a hand on my arm. "Give her some time. She's probably at the old swing set."

Seeing her in pain at what feels like a betrayal is destroying me. Once I tell her the secret I've been keeping, all the ire is likely to be directed at me.

twenty-three

. . .

piper

BETRAYAL DOESN'T EVEN BEGIN to explain what I'm feeling. How dare my parents spring this on us like this. I did think it was weird we didn't do a cookout on Labor Day. Instead, they put it off for a couple of weeks. Just enough time to drop the news and gallivant off to wherever it is they're going.

They may have said where, but I wasn't listening. Not great, I know. But I was trying to process the news. Hell, I'm still trying to process it. The fact they're retiring isn't why I'm upset. We all knew it was coming. It's the timing. They said it would be a few years. Mostly because they have control issues and want to make sure we don't run the business into the ground.

There has to be a reason they are fast tracking this. Something must have happened. Whatever it is, I intend to get to the bottom of it.

I can hear the conversations from the house drifting on

the breeze. They don't sound nearly as upset as I am. They should be. It's even more painful because Parker knew. We've always told each other everything, and this feels like a slap in the face from him especially.

I needed to get away for a bit. Beau got up to follow me, but I'm grateful for whomever told him not to.

There's no clear path I'm taking. Wandering around the property is something I've done since I was a kid. The massive amount of land we own gives me just the right amount of space to think. I can get lost in my head without getting in anyone's way. And, let's face it, if I had stayed on the patio, I probably would have lost my shit on someone.

The sky is darkening and I make my way to the one place I always end up…the swing set from our childhood. Honestly, I'm surprised this thing is still standing. My parents got it when Pierce and Paula were little. We've made so many memories on this thing. I got my first scraped knee after Parker pushed me off the slide because I wouldn't let him have a turn.

I plop down into one of the swings, hoping like hell it doesn't break. Falling to the ground would be the cherry on top of this crappy day.

How can Dad even threaten to sell the winery. Our entire life is on this piece of land. Not only that, we all live here, except for Paula. She does have her own plot of land if she changes her mind. Every milestone, every memory we have is tied to this place. If we can't get along and keep the winery afloat, we'll all have to move. Or have actual property lines drawn up. I can't let that happen.

"I thought I might find you over here." A voice I wasn't expecting comes from behind me.

"Why aren't you eating with everyone else?" He is the family kiss ass after all.

"I didn't much feel like it." Peter sits in the swing next to me. The only difference is, he pushes down on it to make sure it will hold his weight.

"So, you really didn't know Dad was announcing his retirement tonight? I figured being so close to Pierce would make you privy to this sort of information."

He has to feel as betrayed by it all as I do, even if it's not for the same reasons. That's the only reason both of us would be slowly swinging back and forth with our eyes on our feet.

"Yeah, I thought so, too." He shuffles his feet in the dirt, making two tracks.

"It sucks being on this side of information, doesn't it?" It's a dig. I know it as soon as it leaves my mouth. Guilt runs through me at the low blow.

"Yep." I can see his shadow nodding on the ground. "Maybe I've been putting too much of myself into the winery and being at Pierce's beck and call."

"I could have told you that." I snort and swing a bit higher. "You've been so far up his ass since we were kids I didn't know where he ended and you began."

He makes a puking sound. "That is not a great visual. You could have put that more eloquently."

"Not really." I shake my head, but I doubt he sees me. "It's literally the only way to describe your relationship to our elder brother. Take a step back, you might realize you're a completely different person."

Peter sighs. He doesn't say anything, though. Hopefully, he's letting the words resonate. I love all of my siblings, but him and Pierce are the hardest to get along with. Peter is always looking for our big brother's approval, and always managing to fall short.

The only difference between us is it matters to him what Pierce thinks. I don't care, or need approval. Which is why I've been working on the marketing without his knowledge, and quietly taking the wins. I could rub it in his face, but I don't.

I drag my feet to slow myself down. I can't guarantee this swing won't break, and the last thing I want to do is have the seat come out from under me while I'm in the air.

"Do you think we should get back?" He nudges my shoulder once I come to a stop. "I'm sure they'll send out a search party for us."

"You can head back." I nod my head toward the house. One of the things I loved growing up is they put the swing set further away so we could have our own space should we need it. It's like Mom and Dad knew we'd need to come here to find solace. "I'll be up in a minute. Just need to fix my expression and gather my wits."

"Okay, don't be too long or I'll be back to drag you to the house. You need to eat something."

"You act like I haven't been stealing bites the whole time we've been here."

He shakes his head as he stands. "Why am I not surprised? Somehow, you're the only one who gets away with it. At least, without getting your hand smacked."

"Gotta have quick reflexes, big brother." I wave my hands to show how fast they are.

"You are such a dork." He turns back in the direction he came from. "You've got ten minutes. If you aren't at the house, I'll send reinforcements."

I give him a salute before he walks off. Peter may try to

take a step back and focus on himself a bit more, but I don't think he'll ever stop being so bossy. Though, I guess if you think about it, all of us Summers' kids are bossy in our own way. I just hope he knows he's worth more than Pierce will ever let on and do something outside of the winery that makes him happy.

Going back to the house is the last thing I want to do, but Peter is right. I need to go spend time with the family. Even if I'm annoyed with half of them at the moment. Taking the same path Peter did would get me there the fastest, but I still need to make sure my face is hiding any emotions I'm still feeling.

When I get to the fork that will take me to the house or to the metal buildings where all the magic happens, I take a left to go around the buildings. It'll add an extra five minutes. Let Peter come searching for me. He knows I'm not going to be on time unless I absolutely want to.

It's full on dark now, and I'm glad I know this land like the back of my hand. I don't want to use the flashlight on my phone and ruin the serenity I'm starting to feel. There's just something about being out in the open to make your problems seem significantly smaller.

Voices coming from one of the buildings slows my steps. That sounds like Pierce, and…it can't be.

No, I should not eavesdrop on this conversation. It's none of my business. Beau will fill me in on any details later. But…I can't help myself. I tiptoe closer the slightly ajar door. Nobody can say I've never been curious. The trait is usually why I end up in trouble.

"…shouldn't have stormed off like that. Does she have any idea how our parents must feel?" Pierce's voice is angry and I don't blame him. It was a shitty move. Better than turning my frustration out on them, though.

"Maybe you should have given her a heads up," Beau argues. "You know how much she loves this place and your parents." There's silence for a few seconds. Pierce clearly doesn't have anything to say. He doesn't think anyone should know anything until he deems it necessary. "Why are they retiring so soon anyway? I thought that was at least a couple of years away."

I can hear the sigh my brother gives. It sounds tired and defeated. Maybe I shouldn't be so hard on him. He is expected to carry the weight of so much since he's the oldest.

"They've been impressed with the sales and all the work Piper is putting into getting Starlit fields out there. We've doubled our earnings in the time the two of you have been implementing your marketing strategy."

Excuse me, what? This whole time Pierce knew. I've been doing all of this with his approval and didn't know. It's not a bad thing, but still. He shot down my idea when I first presented it to him.

"You need to tell her you've known this whole time. I can't keep this secret any longer." He pauses before taking a deep breath. "It also shouldn't have taken me coming to you about it for you to even consider it."

The gasp that falls from my lips can't be helped. Both of their heads whip toward the door. Shit. I need to get away from here. My feet pound the dirt as I haul ass back to the house with my name falling from Beau's mouth.

Peter is the first person I run into. He puts both hands on my shoulders. "Are you okay? Did you run into a snake or something?"

"C-can you please take me home…right now?" I glance behind my shoulder to see how far behind Beau and Pierce are. "Please, Peter."

"Let's go." He pulls me toward the golf cart and starts it as soon as I slide into the seat. "Is everything okay?"

"No." I take another peek behind me to make sure Beau isn't following me. "And I don't really want to talk about it."

He nods at me and presses the gas pedal to make this thing go as fast as possible. It doesn't take us long to get to my house. I probably could have run the whole way but I know Beau would have caught up and he's the last person I want to see right now.

As soon as he's parked, he turns off the golf cart and waits for me to get out. He's done something he's never done and walks me to my door. Any other time he's gotten me home, he's always just dropped me off and waited until I got inside before peeling out of my driveway. I swear my brother can be a gentleman when he wants to.

The door jingles as I push it open. I completely forgot I have that as my intruder mechanism. "You need to actually lock the damn door. If you're in one of deep sleeps, you'll never hear that."

"I know, I know." One day people will stop riding me about it.

"Do you want me to stay with you?" He knows something is up with Beau, and I'm grateful for his protective big brother act. He's been an unlikely ally tonight, and I love him all the more for it.

"No, I'm good." Before he has a chance to come all the way inside, I add, "And I promise I'll lock the door as soon as I close it. I just want to be alone tonight."

"Okay. Call me if you need anything. I can be here in less than five."

"I will." I start closing the door and stop. "Oh, Peter, thank you for tonight. It really helped with some of what I've been feeling. You're a good big brother."

"I try." He shrugs and backs off my porch. "I'll be back to check on you in the morning."

"It better be with breakfast."

I watch him shake his head as he rushes back to the golf cart. Even though he drives me up the wall, he's there when I really need him. Who knows, our talk tonight could lead to a stronger relationship than we've ever had.

More than anything I want to crawl into bed and figure out how I've been so blind to the fact Beau has been lying to me all along, but I still need to eat dinner. Looks like it's another night of frozen pizza and wine for me. This is why I never open my heart. Even if it is to my best friend. Sadly, I'm not shocked about Pierce's role in all this.

twenty-four

. . .

beau

SHIT. Shit. Shit. This is exactly why I wanted Pierce to tell his sister what was going on sooner than later. Should she have been listening at the door? Probably not. I don't blame her, though.

My feet pound after her. I need to explain. Mostly how it wasn't my idea to keep it a secret. How in the hell is she so fast? I guess fury adds to the adrenaline, and I can't even blame her.

When I finally catch up to her, she's getting into a golf cart with Peter. His eyes narrow on me before he takes off. Unease courses through me. If she's running to the sibling she likes about as much as Pierce, then I've really fucked up.

Honestly, I can't blame anyone but myself. Going to Pierce to begin with was a bad decision. But I knew the repercussions for Piper would be bad if I didn't set up some safety nets for her.

Parker glances at me, his face filled with confusion. I know he wants to ask me what happened, but I'm too busy digging in my pockets searching for my keys. I know for a fact I shoved them in there when I got here for precisely this reason. If Piper wanted to make a quick escape when her family gets to be too much. I never thought she'd be running from me.

I take a step to go around the house, but a hand lands on my shoulder, stopping me in my tracks.

"I may not know my sister as well as you do, but even I know if you go over there right now...she'll rip you to shreds."

"As she should." I whirl on him. "None of this would be a problem if you had given her the chance to prove her methods in the presentation. But no, the almighty Pierce would rather stick his head in the sand instead of building this business to what it could be."

"You have no idea what you're talking about." He argues with his arms crossed over his chest.

The audacity of this guy. I will never understand why he's so different from the rest of his siblings, even Peter isn't as much of an ass.

Before I have a chance to say anything else, someone shoves me. Pierce has the good sense to catch me before I hit the ground. When I turn around Peter is glaring at me. I didn't even hear the golf cart return.

"What the fuck did you do to my sister?"

This isn't behavior I'd expect from him. He's never really paid us much attention. I mean, I know he cares. They are siblings. But I didn't think it was enough to get a rise out of him.

When I don't answer, he takes a step toward me fist

raised. At this point, I would take the ass kicking. I deserve it. I lied to my best-friend, the one person I love more than life itself. I also crossed a line.

Pierce jumps between us. "He's not the only one she's pissed at. Calm the fuck down." The last words are almost a hiss. No doubt trying to keep their parents from coming to investigate.

"What the hell did the two of you do?" Peter's eyes bounce between us. "I'm not surprised she's mad at you." He points at his brother. "But, you." Pointing at me. "Never make her mad. In all the years we've known you, I've never seen the two of you, fight."

"We've never had a reason to…until now." I study the ground in front of me, refusing to make eye contact with Peter. Even if Pierce tries to take some of the heat for this, I'm also to blame.

Pierce gives his brother the information but leaves out the part where if I didn't pull her in, he was going to fire her. Of course, he can't make himself look horrible. Even though he does that on a daily basis with zero help.

"Y'all are really something." Peter shakes his head. "You shouldn't have gone behind her back, Beau. You are the one person Piper trusts in the world. Do you have any idea how this will make her feel?"

"Considering she ran away from me…yeah, I have an idea. Which is why I need to go talk to her." Standing here cementing the fact I fucked up isn't going to make anything better.

"Absolutely not." Peter crosses his arms over his chest. "You need to give her space. When she's ready to talk to you she'll let you know."

How in the hell is he going to dictate when I can talk to

my best friend? It's not like they are even close. She argues with him almost as much as she does Pierce.

"That's not acceptable." I take a step forward. I don't know why. He's not easy to intimidate, but I'm also not going to throw a swing. I wish I could, though. It would feel really freaking good.

"Too bad, Beau." Peter closes the distance between us. "She's hurt because of you and this dumbass." He points toward his brother. "Piper will be fine. I'm bringing her breakfast in the morning."

"Do you even know what she likes?"

"Of course, I do. She's, my sister." Peter turns toward his big brother. "And you are going to let her take off however long she wants. I imagine she wants to talk to you even less than she does Beau. I really thought you learned your lesson after all the bullshit with Paula. But you really can't help being an ass. Can you?"

Pierce's mouth drops open. His brother has never talked to him like this. He usually does whatever he's told and tries to impress Pierce. I guess those days are over.

He doesn't give either of us a chance to respond and marches back to the house. I've seen Peter pissed, but it's usually because we've done something to make Pierce mad. This is the first time I've ever seen him upset on Piper's behalf. He's not wrong, though. Piper will talk to us when she feels like it's right. No matter how much it kills me inside to know I can't do anything to ease the pain. Especially since I'm one of the people who caused it.

There's no point in me being here. "I'm gonna go."

Pierce levels me with a stare. "As long as you're going straight home."

I can't believe he's trying to tell me what to do. He

must have forgotten I'm not one of his siblings. But...I can't argue with his order. If I go over there right now, I have zero doubts she'll rip me a new one.

I know he won't go there either because it'll be ten times worse than whatever I get.

My hands go up in the air in surrender. "I promise I won't stop at Piper's. Can you tell everyone I had to leave?"

It doesn't mean I won't be working on a plan to smooth things over. Maybe she'll be more forgiving after I tell her what Pierce was going to do. Doubt it, though. She'll see it as a betrayal either way. She got hit with two less than great pieces of information tonight. She's not going to take any of this lightly.

"Sure." He nods before turning toward the house and follows his younger brother.

I don't bother waving as I turn toward the side of the house to get to my car. Tonight, did not go the way I intended, but at least now she knows about everything. Not in the way I had planned, but it's all out in the open... mostly.

Instead of going directly to the main road that leads to the winery, I make the loop. I know I said I wouldn't go to Piper's house, but technically I'm not. Driving by is completely different. I only want to make sure she's okay.

The kitchen light casts a yellow glow in her window. It's the only light on in the house from what I can tell. She didn't even get a chance to eat before she left, and I hope she has some food in her freezer. I'd run to town and get her something, but I know it wouldn't help matters.

Leave it to me to completely fuck this up. In over a decade I've never been dishonest with her...until now. I only hope I didn't screw up so badly I put an end to us before we've had a chance to begin.

Knowing she's safe and sound, I pull away from her house and head toward mine. I could go to Out of the Ashes and drown my sorrows for the evening, but I don't deserve the comfort. Not when I've managed to rattle Piper so much in the space of one evening.

The drive home feels like a lost memory. It's like I was at Piper's house then all of a sudden, I was home. I've made the drive so many times it's second nature. This is the first time I've ever felt shame and dejection.

My house is pitch black when I unlock the door. I lock it behind me and head straight to my room. The only thing for me to do is figure out how to make things right.

My phone pings with a text message and I pull it out of my pocket hoping like hell it's Piper. Maybe she's reaching out for my side of the story.

It's not her, though. I flop onto the bed and kick off my shoes.

PARKER

How could you not tell her Pierce knew?

This is not the conversation I feel like having right now, but I guess I need to. It's too long to text so I press his picture and hit call.

"Do you really think it's a good idea to call me right now after everything that went down with my sister?" Well, that's a fun way to answer the phone.

"Hold the judgement. You aren't exactly on her favorite people list either. You didn't tell her about your dad's announcement."

"That's something she'll get over, though." He pauses,

and I can picture him shaking his head. "You, on the other hand, lied to her."

"Who told you about it?" In the end it doesn't really matter, but if he's going to call and bitch me out, he needs to know the full story."

"Pierce. After I asked him where you and Piper were."

"I'm guessing he didn't tell you the part where he threatened to fire Piper?"

He's silent for a long moment and I think he's hung up, but finally he has the outburst I was waiting for. "He did what? He doesn't have the authority to do that. Dad was pretty clear about all of us being a part of the business. Even Paula should she decide to come back."

Parker doesn't interrupt about how this whole thing started after those social stories, and how I needed to keep her from doing them or he'd fire her. It's actually wild when I repeat it. Who the hell does that to a sibling?

"The only way I could prevent that from happening is to tell him we were still going to do it. And he said she couldn't know that he was in on it."

"That's actually fucked up. I would say I can't believe he'd do that, but I can. He's a hard-headed person. I just didn't think he was that stubborn."

"Yeah, he is. He should have just approved her ideas, or at least some of them. It seems like business has been booming since Piper started posting on socials. But I don't even care about Pierce's part in all this. I need to figure out how I'm going to fix things with your sister."

"Please fix it. I don't know that I can handle Piper in a bad mood."

"Have any ideas?" Hopefully he has something

because I don't know what to do. In over ten years we've never really fought.

"Sorry, man. I've got nothing. You are probably the only person who knows her inside and out. She's never really let her full-self shine with the rest of us. Though, that's probably our fault for always picking on her."

"Probably." I sigh in defeat. It took longer than one night for her to find out I was keeping a secret. I need to take more than one night to make things better. Making her mad takes a while, but getting back in her good graces takes even longer. She still doesn't talk to some people in high school over petty things.

"I'll let you know if I think of anything."

"Thanks. Talk to you later." I press the end button and toss my phone on the bed.

I really and truly fucked up with her this time. Tonight, I'll stew in my disappointment. Tomorrow, though, it's time to figure out how I'm going to get my girl back. Even if it's not in a romantic way, I need my best friend.

twenty-five

. . .

piper

THREE DAYS. That's how long it's been since I've talked to anyone in my family other than Peter. I never thought he'd be one to have my back the way he has the past few days. Him being in my corner is much appreciated, even if he didn't vouch for me when I initially presented the marketing plan. There's always room for growth.

There's a knock at my door and I pause the music I have blasting through the living room while I stress clean.

I don't bother looking as I open it. "Peter, I'm fine. I don't need any more food."

Except he's not the person on my porch. It's my sister. "Well, I guess you're shit out of luck because I'm here with food."

Opening the door wider, I motion her to come inside. "At this rate, I'm going to be waddling into work when I go back."

It's mostly the paperwork I'll need to get done. Despite

all the drama surrounding the social media blasts, I'm still doing them. They are what is driving business and there's no reason it should stop. If anything, I'm doing it to rub it in Pierce's face.

"You weren't answering my texts, or calls. I needed to come by and do a proof of life check. And to make sure you weren't lying on the couch drowning your sorrows in sangria."

"Please, as if I would allow myself to do that."

Paula lifts an eyebrow. "Yes, you would, you have a habit of being dramatic when it benefits you."

She's not wrong. It's the only way I could get my way on some things when I was younger because nobody would listen to me. I did storm off during the cookout, so maybe she has a point.

"What did you bring to eat?" I try to pull the bag from her hands and she shoos me away.

I'm actually glad she's here. She hasn't always gotten along with Pierce so she won't judge me too harshly on anything I want to vent about. But…she's also the only sibling in a relationship and I need to pick her brain.

"Wings. Eric also said to stop moping and come see him at the bar." She shakes her head in exasperation. The feeling is mutual. As one of the best bartenders Out of the Ashes has, he's always in everyone's business. It's kind of annoying, actually.

"How does he know I'm moping?"

"I'm not sure. He mentioned something about Beau being sad last night, and assumed since you weren't with him, you were, too."

"That man is way too perceptive." I sit on the couch and lower the music. "Have you talked to Beau?"

She nods before bringing the boxes with the food to the living room. I have a perfectly good kitchen table, but eating on the couch is much more comfortable.

"He's definitely not happy right now. And, he's pissed at himself for not saying anything sooner."

I grab a wing and dip it into ranch. He's not the only one who's miserable. I haven't slept well since the cook-out. I keep reaching for my phone to reply to his texts, but decide not to every single time.

"We've never gone this long without talking. Even when we go on our business building trips, we keep in touch."

"Y'all need to fix this. I don't know how to handle the two of you." I open my mouth, but she raises her hand to stop me. "I'm not saying you have to forgive him right this second. But give him a chance to tell his side of the story. You can't rely on a snippet of conversation you overheard. You may not know all the details."

Of course she's defending Beau. But it makes me wonder what I don't know. It's bad enough he kept things a secret, but maybe it was for a good reason. He probably thought he was protecting me from something. It's the same thing he used to do when we were in high school and he was worried I would hear whatever rumors the popular crowd was spreading.

"Do I need to keep that same energy for Pierce?"

"Hell no." She laughs. "He shouldn't have shot down your idea to begin with. All the work you and Beau have done has boosted the winery. He needs to listen to the younger siblings. You have a pulse on what people your age want."

I never thought about it like that. There are tons of

things people in town want to do, but they have to drive to the closest city to do it. Which is making my brain turn with more ideas. We can bring some of those things to our area. I need to write these things down before I forget them. Well, put them in my phone.

"What are you doing?" Paula asks as I look for my phone.

"You spurred some ideas." I find it stuck between the couch cushions. My fingers fly across the screen as I think of events we could have at the winery. "And some of them may be great to have you on board."

"No, no, no." She waves her hands in front of her. "You're not completely roping me back into the winery."

"No, nothing like that." I shake my head and keep typing. "Similar to that party you did, but on a smaller scale. I'm thinking craft nights, and shop and sips. Things to bring the community together while also supporting small business."

"Oh, that I can get down with. We could also do a floral arranging night."

Yes, she's getting on the same wavelength as me. "I love it. Then it's promoting Starlit and Whoopsie Daisy."

"These are the ideas Pierce needs to be listening to." Paula bumps into me with her shoulder. "The winery can't go wrong with you leading the marketing." She takes a bite of her salad. "By the way, how did you avoid Pierce seeing the posts you were doing?"

"I blocked him."

"Smart." She taps her finger to her temple.

It was the only way I could ensure he wouldn't figure out what I was doing. Even though apparently, he already knew. I can't believe I let them play me like that. I can usually spot the bullshit from a mile away. It's the whole reason all of my dates usually end before they even begin.

"So, you think I should give Beau a chance to explain himself?" I've never been unsure of anything. Beau has also never lied to me. This feels worse than hearing Dad is retiring now and some of the siblings knowing about it.

As bad as it sounds, I expected that. There are always things being hidden within our family despite how open we are with each other. Somehow knowing something the others don't feels like having the upper hand. When there are six of us, it's kind of the norm.

She rolls her eyes. "I swear sometimes you can be so dense."

"What's that supposed to mean?" I know I should be offended, but she has a point. I'm just as stubborn as Pierce once I've made my mind up about something. I haven't, though…not yet.

"It means you need to talk to him. He's your best friend, Piper. The one person you turn to for everything. Are you willing to throw away over a decade of friendship without letting him say his piece?"

Am I? The thought of never speaking to him again sends a pang of pain through my entire body. He is my calm through the madness of dealing with my siblings. The person I have more fun with than anyone I've ever known. Beau has always had my back whether or not I was in the right. He stands by me through everything. But he lied to me…for weeks.

"I don't know if I can continue dating him, though. Not if he's going to keep things from me."

Paula wraps an arm around my shoulder, my food is all but forgotten. It's fine. I wasn't that hungry anyway.

Not with the way Peter has been bringing all of my favorite foods the past couple of days. I didn't even realize he knew what I liked. He's more perceptive than I thought.

"Baby sister, that's something you'll have to figure out for yourself." One last squeeze. "If I were you, I wouldn't make any decisions until I knew the whole story. There could be a valid reason for him not saying anything."

"I guess."

"Well, I have to get back to work." She picks up her food box and puts it back in the bag. Then she grabs mine and takes it to the kitchen, placing it in the fridge.

"Can I go with you?" God, I sound like a child. Now that I've had her here with me, I don't want her to leave.

"Um, no. But give me just a second." She pulls her phone out of her pocket and heads toward the hallway. I'm guessing she wants a little privacy for whatever call she's about to make.

To keep myself occupied, I check over the ideas I put in my phone moments ago. These are solid, and I swear if Pierce doesn't listen to me, I may hit him. My methods have proved to be profitable. This will only increase it.

"Good news," Paula says as she comes back into the living room. "The girls gave me the rest of the day off. So, I'm all yours." She veers off to the kitchen and grabs a bottle of wine.

"Weren't you just making sure I wasn't day drinking?" I shake my head as she comes back with two glasses and the bottle. "And why are you drinking? The other day you said you couldn't. Now you need to spill the beans since we're done with boy talk."

"Are you sure we're done? I'm sure there's more we could say."

"Yes, I'm sure. Now tell me what's going on."

She pours the wine into the glasses and hands me one before scooting into the corner of the couch. "I thought I might have been pregnant."

"Oh my gosh. Are you serious?" I nod toward the glass in her hand. "I'm guessing you're not."

"No, I'm not. I've just been stressed with learning the flower arrangements and living with someone that my period was later than normal."

"Are you disappointed?" Even though she's been putting on a happy face for me, she seems sad.

"Yes? No?" She throws a hand up in the air. "I don't know. We aren't actively trying. But a part of me wondered how it would feel to start a family. At the same time, he's busy with Crooked Halo, and business at the shop is booming. Having a kid right now would not be a good idea. Plus, we really haven't been together long."

"That's valid." I reach over and place my hand on her leg. "It'll happen when it's time. For now, enjoy the time the two of you have. Who knows, maybe you'll have a whole bunch of kids to match Mom and Dad."

"Oh, hell no." She takes a big gulp of her wine. "There's no way I'm having that many kids. I love you all, but I don't have the patience for that. Can you imagine me trying to keep six kids in line?" She shakes her head and laughs. "I honestly don't know how Mom did it."

"She's a saint. And Dad was a lot of help."

"You're right. It's still a hard pass for me." She grabs the remote off the coffee table and finds a streaming service. "Let's watch a movie. It's been forever since we've hung out like this without everyone else."

She's right. We haven't. "Pick whatever you want."

Spending time with Paula and Peter on their own has been refreshing. I'm used to hanging out with Parker because we're closer in age. Even if things work out with me and Beau, I'm making a vow right now to spend one on one time with each of my siblings. Even Pierce. Maybe we'll all get to understand each other better.

Now I only need to decide if I'm going to reach out to Beau, or wait for him to come see me and talk to me in person.

twenty-six

. . .

beau

MY PLAN IS IN PLACE. Parker assured me his sister was coming into work this week. I don't think I've ever not talked to Piper for this long. It's weird having all this time to myself. But it made me realize a few things and none of them are as important as having her in my life.

I send Parker and Pierce a quick text.

BEAU

Is everything set up?

They have to make sure everything is set up because I don't want to get there and run into Piper. Not until she sees this. Not until I have a chance to explain what happened. I could give a rat's ass if Pierce has given her his side. From what I've heard from Parker he's not telling everyone the whole story. Today…she'll hear it from me.

PARKER

You're good to go. Park at my house and I'll come get you in the golf cart. It's the only way she won't see you.

PIERCE

I'll keep her occupied in the office. She wants to redesign the shipping boxes. That should keep us busy for a while.

BEAU

See you in a bit. I'll send Parker a text when I'm ready.

I shove my phone in my pocket and grab the sticky notes off my counter. Wait, I need a pen, too. I think there's one in my car, but I'm not taking any chances. This whole thing needs to go off without a hitch.

The drive to Parker's house doesn't take me long. There's a possibility I pushed the speed limit to get here. I think I'm more nervous now than I was when I kissed her. It'll be worth it though. Even if she doesn't want to continue being my girlfriend, I need her as my friend. A life without Piper in it in some capacity is dull and boring. One I don't want.

Parker is already waiting in the golf cart when I pull in. "Are you ready for this?" The question comes as soon as I open my car door.

"Yeah. They set it up far enough away that she won't see it until you bring her, right?" I bend down and grab my supplies. It's important that I leave notes along the way, or she'll take forever to find me.

"Of course." He puts his hand over his chest as if the question hurt him. "I'm not an amateur." He starts the golf cart and we take off as fast as it can go. "I do need the two of you to kiss and make up, though. Seeing both of you miserable is not fun."

"No shit." Of course, Parker will make it about him. But I get it. I've been a part of their lives for a long time. It can't be easy for them to feel the rift between me and Piper.

The ride is bumpy as we move over the open fields. He doesn't take us close to the main house where all the business is conducted. There are too many points where she could look out the window and see us. Instead, he heads to the far end of the land and takes us behind the buildings before pulling up to the fun house.

"This is such a weird idea. Why a fucking fun house? Those things are creepy."

"Because your sister likes them. She's never told me why, but she does. I'm just lucky they were available on such short notice."

"Of course they were. It's the middle of the week. He did say to call him as soon as we can, he has to hit the road for another fair tonight." He points to opening. "I put a speaker, blanket, food and wine up there. I think I got everything you requested."

"Thanks, man. Seriously, you've been a big help in getting this together for me."

"It's all good. How long do you want me to give you to set up?"

I glance at the notes in my hand and at the fun house. "Ten minutes. Can you get the generator going while I set up inside?"

"Sure thing."

Both of us get out of the golf cart. He heads around the

side toward the back, and I head for the front door. Each note will lead her straight to me.

I place one on the entrance before picking up the supplies. At least he put it all in a basket. Otherwise, this would be a lot harder. After walking in, I take a left and set another note. The lights come on and I can hear the generator hum as I make my way through to the mirrors. I've placed notes along the way and when I get to my destination, I set everything down.

I lay the blanket out and shove the basket behind one of the walls. There are a couple of seat cushions and I set those across from each other before pouring two glasses of wine. This will either go amazing or she'll throw the wine in my face.

Now, all I can do is wait. Parker should be on his way to get his sister. I don't know how he is going to get her to leave whatever she's working on. But I'm hoping when she see's everything, she'll hear me out.

Twenty minutes pass by and I'm almost convinced she's not coming. It serves me right. I did fuck this up. I should have listened to my gut and told her everything from the beginning. The fear of Pierce finding out and her losing her job was too much, though.

I know her brother can't technically do that. Especially after what their dad said at the cookout the other day. They are all in, or he's selling. It's a drastic move, but I'm glad it won't give Pierce the ability to do whatever he wants without consequence. Although, it'd be a bad idea to get rid of Piper now that business is picking up thanks to her efforts.

My phone vibrates against the floor. Please don't be a text saying she's not coming. We've texted a little this week, but it's been very surface level. Nothing too deep and mostly gifs of puppies. That's Piper's go to when she's not feeling great, or everything feels like too much.

I unlock my phone and glance at the text.

PARKER

She's heading in. Good luck.

Hmm, why do I need luck? This doesn't bode well for the course of the day. I'm not going to reply and ask him to elaborate. I'll find out as soon as she makes her way back here.

Another ten minutes pass. What is taking her so long? It didn't even take me this long to set up. Maybe it's nerves. I stand in the mirrored hallway before pacing back and forth. I've never been nervous to see Piper. Well, except for the last time we were in this space. This is a thousand times worse, though. Everything hangs in the balance.

"Beau?" My name on Piper's lips stops me in my tracks and I turn to face her. "What is all this?" She waves her hands around to encompass the fun house.

"The beginning of an apology?" Shit. That wasn't supposed to come out as a question. How is she supposed to take me seriously if I sound unsure?

"I assumed that much." Her steps are slow and deliberate as she comes closer to me. "But why?"

I can't tell her it's because we've watched enough rom-coms for me to know I need to do something big. She may act like she doesn't want all the focus on her, but I know it's a lie. All she's ever wanted was her siblings to see her for the amazing person she is. I want, no need, her to know that I see her.

"Because you love fun houses, and I thought it was the perfect place to tell you how sorry I am."

I back up as she comes closer, not wanting to scare her off. I take a seat on the far corner of the blanket and wait for her to sit down. She takes a moment to glance around at everything I've done. The bright yellow of the sticky notes stand out in this dimly lit space.

"You lied to me, Beau." She sets down the notes and clasps her hands together. But she doesn't look at me. "We've never lied to each other."

"I know." I study the wine bottle so she doesn't see the shame written across my face. "I had a good reason, though."

She throws her hands in the air. I don't blame her, I'd be frustrated, too. "That's the thing. We've always been honest with each other no matter how bad the information is. What in the hell was so detrimental that you couldn't tell me the truth?"

I've never seen her like this. She's never cussed at me, and I know for a fact I don't want her to ever do that again. Not that it's not deserved. It is, one hundred percent. But it doesn't feel great.

"Pierce." It's the only word I can come up with for the moment. At least until I can find the words to tell her exactly what was said that won't make her angrier.

"Yes, I know Pierce was part of this whole thing. He knew the entire time, but I don't see why you couldn't tell me anything."

Well, there's no way she's not going to be pissed. I guess I need to come out and say it.

"He was going to fire you."

"For what?" She lifts her head until her eyes meet

mine. "Up until this weekend, he couldn't do it if he wanted."

I rub the bridge of my nose and sigh. "After we posted those stories, the night you kissed me. He called me the next day. He told me I needed to keep you from posting anything or he'd fire you."

Her gasp sends a bullet through my heart. "I don't understand."

The whispered disbelief doesn't ease the pain. I reach forward and place my hand on top of hers, lending her the strength I know she's going to need.

"When I came over to help your family clean up after the storm, I talked to him. I knew you wanted to keep going with the marketing, and my boss wanted to see what we could do. The only way I could make sure that happened was if I went to him and told him we were going to boost social media marketing. I told him the plans."

"And I'm guessing he said okay to you." She shakes her head. "Unbelievable. He wouldn't give me the time of day, but he didn't even fight you on it."

She yanks her hand from mine and stands, staring at her reflection in the mirror. The look on her face is the reason I didn't want to tell her. She looks like someone just stole her puppy. Her fear of being rejected by those she loves pouring from her eyes.

I'm on my feet in two seconds, moving behind her. "Piper, look at me." She lifts her eyes until they meet mine reflected in the mirror. "This is why I didn't want to tell you the truth."

"You should have, though. This is so unfair. He lets everyone else give him their opinions but not me. Hell, he even relented to Paula's idea. What is so wrong with me that nobody listens to me?"

I'm done talking to her reflection. My hand reaches for her again, and I turn her around. She refuses to meet my eyes until I lift her chin. She needs to know how fucking special she is and it doesn't matter what her dickhead brother thinks.

"I will always listen to you." A few strands of hair fall to her face and I tuck them behind her ear. My thumb caresses her skin to bring her back to the moment as her focus drifts to her shoes. "If it makes you feel any better, I told him he's an asshole for shooting down your idea. And I shouldn't have had to step in on your behalf."

Her eyes snap back to mine. "You did what?"

twenty-seven

. . .

piper

I CAN'T BELIEVE he called my brother out on his bullshit. Nobody else, besides Paula, has ever really done that. Sure, they've talked shit about him when he's not around. But nothing like what Beau did. And they sure as hell didn't stand up for me.

"I told him he was a dumbass. You have so many great ideas, and there wouldn't be the massive growth the winery is seeing without you."

Paula was right. I needed to hear his side of the story. I haven't even talked to Pierce about this whole ordeal. We've kept it strictly business since I came back to the office. He's going to wish he had fessed up to me about this when I see him again.

"Thank you." My voice is barely above a whisper.

"So, are we good? Do you forgive me? Because as much as I love sharing puppy gifs with you, I miss my friend. I miss my girlfriend. You have no idea how much this has been eating me up inside."

Do I forgive him? He should have told me all this from the beginning. I'm not sure why he thought I wouldn't find out. My family is a lot of things, but good at keeping secrets isn't one of them. Although, I don't think any of them knew about the threat of being fired or that Pierce actually knew about it this whole time.

"Clearly not enough to break down and tell me. Instead, I had to find out from overhearing the two of you."

Is it a bitchy come back? Yes. Do I regret it? Not at all. Even if I was already leaning toward forgiving him after my talk with Paula, he doesn't need to know that. He can squirm for a bit.

"I know. You have no idea how sorry I am." Now he's looking at the mirror behind me. The only reason I know is because I can see his reflection. "I've been a mess at work all week. And I turned down the promotion."

"What? Why?" We were supposed to discuss it that night, but then everything happened and it slipped my mind.

"Because I don't want to have to choose between working long hours and spending time with you. That position would have never brought me the joy I get from being near you, or working with businesses who actually need my help."

He leans his forehead against the glass, caging me between him and the mirror. I don't push him away. "I would have never made you choose."

"I know." His voice is soft. "I'm putting money back to go out on my own, but not in the way I've been working at the firm. I want to help people figure out their strengths to make their business a success without throwing a bunch of money at it. I'll never be able to do that where I'm at now."

Now he leans back and meets my eyes. "You are my success story. Not just in business, but also in life. You are the only person who has ever shown me unconditional love, and not treated me like I'm a burden."

Well, shit. What am I supposed to say to that? Nothing.

I throw my arms around him and pull his lips down to mine, doing the one thing I've wanted to do all week. Yes, I was pissed, but deep down I knew he was doing what he thought was right…for me.

He pulls back and grins. "So, I guess we're okay."

"Yes, we're okay." I walk him backward until we are on the blanket and push him until he's sitting on the blanket. I straddle him and place my hands on the mirror on either side of him. "But if you ever lie to me again, I don't think I could come back from that."

"Never again." He groans as I grind into him.

He reaches for my shorts, trying to undo the button, and I push his hand away. "Not yet."

I leave a trail of kisses along his neck before my lips join his once more. It's probably wrong to torture him like this, but it serves him right. His hand wanders all over my body. Caressing. Gripping. Each touch a sign of how much he wants me.

My hands find their way to his jeans and I unbutton them, ready to put him out of his misery. He doesn't hesitate undoing the button on my shorts and I lift up enough to help him work their way down my legs and he kicks off his own.

The sound of glass tinkles in the background, barely

audible over the music playing on the speaker. Oh well, we can worry about that mess later.

"Shit," Beau hiss and scrambles for his jeans. He pulls his wallet out of the pocket and produces a condom. At least he's always prepared.

He tries to lean me back so I can lie down, but I yank the condom out of his hand and slide it over him. He groans as I lower myself on him and his head falls back hitting the mirror with a soft thud.

I rock my body into him while bending down to kiss him. I expect him to close his eyes, but he doesn't. He's focused on the mirrors and watching the two of us from every angle. I'd be lying if I said it didn't turn me on.

His hands grip my hips, quickening the pace. My hands drag down the mirrors as I keep myself steady and I break the kiss. Wanting to see what he does.

Passion and love. The awe on his face as he watches me watch him. If I needed proof that he sees me, this moment is it. Beau gets me on a level nobody ever has. He knows when to be strong for me, and when I need to be the strong one.

His grip tightens as the pressure builds and we're both tumbling into our release. That has never happened before and I hope like hell this isn't the last time.

"I love you, Piper." The words are breathless as he tries to catch his.

"I love you, too." I give him a quick peck before climbing off him. I search around in the dim light for my shorts and use the edge of the blanket to clean myself off.

Beau cleans up while I get dressed and start cleaning up the spilled wine. At this point, we should probably throw away the blanket. Those sangria stains are never coming out of there.

His hand covers mine until I give him my full attention. "No, I really love you."

"I know." And I do. He proves it in the way he's always taken care of me. Met my needs before I even realized I needed them. He feeds me because he knows I can't cook. All those small things have shown me just how much this man loves me.

Without another word he helps me clean up the mess we've made. Once everything is inside the basket he pulled from some hiding place, he pulls me toward him. "I think fun houses are my new favorite attraction. You've helped me create some pretty amazing memories."

"For sure. Also, how do you feel about adding mirrors to our bedrooms?"

"I'm not opposed." He brings his lips to mine. We stand there, wrapped up in each other, tongues dancing, enjoying the moment. Enjoying us and knowing everything is going to be okay.

"Good." I check around the area to make sure everything is cleaned up. I'm sure he paid a pretty penny to rent this thing, but I'm not going to ask him how much. It's not business. "Now, I need to find my big brother."

Thank God Parker left the golf cart. Though I can't believe he walked all the way back to the main house. It's way too hot for that.

"Where's Pierce?" I don't bother hiding my anger as I stomp into the office.

Parker looks me up and down before shaking his head. "You were gone way too long to be coming in here with that much attitude."

"Just tell me where our big brother is." I roll my eyes and put my hands on my hips. It's the same stance I've taken since I was a child and wouldn't take no for an answer.

"Beau?" Parker asks as if looking for approval.

I glance behind me to see what Beau's reaction is.

His hands are up as if he wants nothing to do with this conversation. "This has nothing to do with me. And she really needs to talk to Pierce."

"I guess I better prepare for the battle that's about to happen." Parker sighs and stands up. "I think he's in the stock building. Please don't break any of the merchandise."

"I'm not dumb, Parker."

I turn to head out of the office and Beau stops me. "Do you want me to go with you?"

Shaking my head, I give him a quick hug. "This is something I need to do on my own. It's time I take a page out of my sister's book and stand up to him."

"Good luck." He kisses the top of my head and lets me go.

That is the support I need right now and I'm grateful he has my back. Parker can stuff it. I have a feeling he's going to follow me up there, though. Not to offer a helping hand, but so he can hear the details and tell the rest of the siblings. He's so freaking nosey. Can I really blame him, though? When you have this many siblings, it's best to know everyone's secrets.

Pierce is putting together boxes when I open the door. I

make sure it slams shut behind me. If Parker wants to know what's going on, he'll have to work for it.

"Can you tell me why my marketing plan was a good idea when it came from Beau and not me?"

"No, I can't." He's not even raising his voice. What the hell is going on?

"Seriously, that's all you have to say? Especially after you told Beau you were going to fire me if I didn't stop live posting."

"I was wrong." Not a single emotion.

My shoes thud against the concrete as I stomp to the work table and slap my hands on top of it. "Dammit, Pierce, give me a real answer because you have no idea how bad it hurts to be shot down by my own brother. Then turn around and find out he okayed it when it came from a man."

Now he meets my eyes and there's a sadness in them. "I didn't think you could handle the pressure. You've always been one to come up with these big ideas, but when they don't work out, you're crushed. I didn't want you to fail."

"It was the same exact plan Beau mentioned." I point toward the door because I'm sure he followed Parker behind me. "We worked on it together. So, if you didn't want me to fail what the hell changed your mind?"

Pierce runs a hand through his hair and glances at the ceiling as if asking a higher power for patience. "I saw it was working. After you made those stories replying to questions, the orders came pouring in. I knew the reason."

"Then why not tell me you were approving the plan? All of this could have been avoided."

"Because I'm stubborn. It's a shitty reason, I know. But

there it is." He sets the box he was building aside and leans his elbows on the table. "I'm supposed to be someone you look up to, and I keep fucking up at every turn. How am I supposed to run this business when I can't realize what is a good time investment and what isn't?"

Whoa. I didn't realize how stressed he's been about Dad retiring. I'm sure the accelerated time frame isn't helping matters. Now I feel kind of bad for him.

"Last time I checked, there are six of us. Dad never meant for you to be the one making all the decisions. You're at the top because you're the oldest. But the rest of us can also carry some of that burden." Well, except Paula, but I don't mention her. She'll come back into the fold when she's ready.

"You shouldn't have to, though."

"Stop being a baby and let us take some of it on. It's not like you're going to win a prize for being the best boss and most asshole brother."

"I should if there was actually an award for that."

"Look, what you did was shitty. I'll eventually forgive you for it. But…don't toss aside my ideas because I'm the youngest. I do actually know what I'm talking about from time to time."

I move around the table and give my brother a hug. Mom always made us do it when we got in disagreements as kids, and it seems like he might need some comfort.

"I'll try." He hugs me back.

"Good."

Do I think he'll change overnight? Not a chance in hell, but maybe he'll actually work on not being such a dick.

"Aw, everyone has made up." Parker runs to us and

wraps his arms around the both of us. "Get in here, Beau. You're pretty much family, too."

Beau joins us, but his arms are only around me. It's going to take a while for Pierce to get back in his good graces.

This is part of having a big family, though. We may fight and disagree most of the time, but we can move mountains when we stick together. I just hope my big brother realizes it or it might bite him in the ass.

"You wanna get out of here?" Beau whispers in my ear.

"Absolutely." I pull us out of the huddle. "I'm taking the rest of the day off."

"You literally just came back yesterday."

"Consider it payback for being an asshole." I wave behind me as I pull Beau with me toward the door. I can practically hear my brother's eyes roll, but he doesn't try to stop me.

We have a lot of making up to do, and I want him to tell me all about his plan to leave the firm he works for. Despite all the ups and downs, he's still my best friend, even if he's also my boyfriend, and I'll support him the way he's always supported me.

epilogue

. . .

one year later

"WHY AM I WEARING A BLINDFOLD?" Piper shifts uncomfortable as I drive away from her house.

"Because I have a surprise for you." This is something I've been working on for the past month. It's a good thing we live in a small town and Starlit Fields makes large donations to the school district. Otherwise…I never would have been able to pull this off.

"Did you finally get an office space so you can stop working out of your living room?" Her voice is filled with excitement and it's contagious.

I left the firm six months ago. Now I help small businesses make their mark on social media and small-scale events to get their name out there. It's turned more into coaching. While I don't make quite as much as I did at the firm, I'm happy. This is my passion and I couldn't have done it without Piper's encouragement and support.

"Not yet." I chuckle. "But I have an idea for that coming soon."

"Well, are you going to tell me about it?"

"Not yet."

"Fine." She crosses her arms over her chest.

I know she's trying to go for angry, but it's adorable. Mostly because I can see the small lift of her lip while she tries to hide a smile.

She sighs and reaches for the radio. She misses the button and accidentally hits the air condition knob.

"Would you stop fidgeting? We're almost there."

"This is a good surprise, right?" She moves her hands to play with her hair at the ends of her braid. "Last time there was a surprise it caused a whole thing. I don't want to argue with anyone today."

"It's a good surprise. Have a little faith in me."

"I actually have a lot of faith in you. Don't ruin it."

I come to a stop down the road from Starlit Fields Winery. The place our story began. After turning off the car, I unbuckle my seatbelt. "Stay right there. I'm coming to lead you out of the car."

"Okay," she holds her hands up. "I won't move."

That lasts all of ten seconds. By the time I make it to her door, she's unbuckled her seatbelt and is reaching for the handle to open it. "You are so impatient."

"You wouldn't have me any other way."

She's right. It's one of the things I love about her.

I glance at the yellow school bus pulled to the side of the road in front of us. Our family fills as many of the seats as they can except for one. Parker is trying to get everyone to be quiet. Paula waves the bouquet in her hands. I'm putting it all on the line right now and I hope like hell everything plays out the way I'm hoping.

Our steps to the bus are slow. She's wearing wedges and I keep trying to lead her while not throwing her off balance. Once we're to the doors, I stop. "I'm going to carry you for a bit. Wrap your arms around my neck and don't let go."

"Um, okay. This is weird, but I'll go with it...for now."

As soon as her arms are secured around me, I lift her around her waist making sure her feet aren't going to hit the steps. This is harder than I thought it would be. I don't want her to figure out where we are just yet.

"Why does it smell like a gym locker room?"

Damn. I probably should have had the bus barn air it out a bit. It's too late for that now.

Philip stands behind me and guides me backward until we're in front of the exact seat we were in on the day we met. Turning, I slide Piper into the seat. She lifts her hands to the blindfold, but I wrap my fingers around her wrist. "Not yet."

"Okay, but whatever I'm sitting on feels vaguely familiar."

"Because it is."

Paula hands me the bouquet and Peter hands me the book I was reading on the day that forever changed my life. Pierce stands in the aisle with his phone held up and gives me a thumbs up.

"You can lift the blindfold now."

She doesn't waste any time ripping it off her head and her eyes widen at scene before us. "Wh—what is this?"

I hand her the bouquet. And she stares at them before looking over at me and the book in my hand.

"Is this the bus we rode when we were in school?"

"Yep. Though the seats seem a hell of a lot smaller."

"Why is my family here?"

Setting the book down, I slide off the seat and do my best to get down on one knee. I'll regret this tomorrow because I can see sticky areas all over the floor.

"Piper, this is the day I fell in love with you. Even though I acted annoyed with having to share my seat, you showed me nothing but kindness. You became my best friend after that one interaction. I knew in that moment I didn't want to spend a day of my life without you. Most people don't believe in soulmates, but I know for a fact you are mine. We may not have always made the best decisions, but we always stuck by each other."

Her free hand moves to her mouth, and her eyes are watery.

"Will you do me the honor of making poor decisions and backing each other up for the rest of our lives?"

"Yes!"

She tries to toss the bouquet, but I grab it before it flies over the seat. There are ten white roses surrounding a yellow and red one in the center. Those are the two I pull out. Tied between is the engagement ring her mom helped me pick out.

"These symbolize us." I say as I untie the string and let the ring fall into my hand. "We will always be friends first. It's the foundation of our relationship, and know I will love you every day just as much as I did when we were thirteen."

Piper holds her hand out and I slip the ring onto her finger. Her family claps and cheers in the background as

Piper throws her arms around me nearly knocking me to the floor.

"I love you, Beau."

"I love you, too."

She kisses me long and hard, not caring that we're surrounded by her siblings. At least, until Parker starts making gagging noises as if he's going to throw up.

She sits up and pulls me with her. "I'm not even going to ask what strings you pulled to make this happen. But can we please get off this bus? It smells like school memories."

"Hey, they weren't all bad." I grab her hand and help her out of the seat.

"No, they weren't." She squeezes my hand as I lead her off the bus. "They brought me you."

"I need a drink." Parker announces as they file off after us.

Pierce puts his phone back in his pocket. "I've got a spread set up on the back patio."

"We'll meet you there." I wave as they all head to their cars. "Oh, Peter, can you call the bus barn and let them know we're done with the bus."

"You've got it." He presses a button on his phone as he slides into the truck with Pierce.

Piper turns toward me, stars in her eyes. "Thank you."

"For what?" I pull her closer to me.

"All this and having my family be a part of it."

"They're my family too." I laugh before kissing her forehead. "And when are you going to realize, I would do anything for you."

"We aren't even married yet, and you're spoiling me with all my favorite memories."

"And it's never going to stop." I wrap my arms around her waist and mold my lips to hers. This feels like home and family. Things I never thought I'd have, but Piper gave me.

248

acknowledgments

It truly takes a village to write a book. I couldn't have done it without Stephanie, Alex, and Ashley. They are my ride or dies. Anytime I felt like I couldn't do it, they were there cheering me on. Thank you for being a part of my life. I seriously don't know what I'd do without talking to y'all every day.

Wee One, the way you keep me on track is a little scary. Thank you for making sure I'm doing what I'm supposed to and not binge watching *Supernatural* or *Doctor Who* again.

Boy Child and the Grand, you two keep me on my toes. Anytime I need a laugh, you're there to supply it.

Hubs, I love you! Your support means the world to me, and I honestly couldn't write my heroes if it weren't for you.

My parents…thanks for listening to me yap about my books. Y'all have been my biggest support system since day one. I love y'all!

Claudia, thank you for being the best Alpha reader. Seriously, you notice the things I don't and I'm forever grateful for you.

Last but not least, readers. Thank you for your continued support. Some of you have been with me since the beginning, and some of you are new. Thank you for reading my words and connecting with my characters. You truly make this the easiest job ever.

also by katrina marie

Do you want to meet more of the characters in Asheville? You can check out my books here. Or, scan the QR code to find out what some of the other residents of this small town are up to.

about the author

Katrina Marie lives in the Dallas area with her husband, two children, and fur baby. She is a lover of all things geeky and Gryffindor for life. When she's not writing you can find her at her children's sporting events, or curled up reading a book.

You can find Katrina Marie online in the following places:

Sign up for my newsletter: https://katrinamarieauthor.com/newsletter

Website: katrinamarieauthor.com

facebook.com/katrinamarieauthor

instagram.com/katrinamarieauthor

bookbub.com/profile/katrina-marie

pinterest.com/katrinamarieauthor

www.ingramcontent.com/pod-product-compliance
Lightning Source LLC
Chambersburg PA
CBHW061805190726
48289CB00007B/2074